UNQUENCHABLE

THE SERENDIPITY DUET – BOOK TWO

TAWDRA KANDLE

Unquenchable
Copyright © 2014 Tawdra Kandle

All rights reserved.

ISBN-978-1-68230-261-3

To Amanda, who keeps me on the straight and narrow when it comes to alcohol, certain words and safe sex. You make my books infinitely better and you make me a better writer. And you make me laugh until I cry.

Thank you for all of that.

PROLOGUE

FIRST THERE WAS BLOOD. Then there was pain. And then there was darkness, and in the darkness, there was peace. There was no sense of being or time, just darkness.

And then there was a light, and someone standing by the bed where I lay.

"Nell."

She spoke my name, and I blinked, disoriented. My eyes could not focus on the woman addressing me.

"Don't try to talk. You have been asleep for quite a long time, and you need to recover."

She smiled, just slightly. I closed my eyes, and when I opened them again, I could see her more clearly. She had blonde hair so pale it was nearly white. It was pulled back from her face. My vision focused a little more, and I saw that her eyes were a vivid blue. They met mine with interest.

"I'm Cathryn Whitmore. You don't know me, but I promise, I'm a friend."

My mind began to function again, and a few memories filtered back in. I sucked in a breath as scenes flitted across my brain.

Tasmyn. Marica.

Cathryn touched my hand as understanding flashed in her eyes. "Tasmyn is fine. You saved her, or at least you held off Marcia Lacusta until Tasmyn could save herself. She is well, I promise. I just saw her last week."

I furrowed my forehead, and the movement felt odd, off, as if my body weren't quite my own yet. A lock of my long black hair fell across my face, but I didn't have the strength to reach up and move it away.

Marica. Where is she? What happened? Is she ... gone?

"Yes." Cathryn nodded, and it dawned on me that she was answering what I couldn't say. I had some familiarity with that particular talent, though it wasn't my own.

"Marica was taken into custody by the local police, and since those happened to be the police of King, who are accustomed to dealing with magic when it goes wrong, she was sent away. Held in an institute for a short period of time, until someone from her own ... ah ... tribe came to take her home. She's in Romania now, in the custody of her family."

My heart beat just a little faster, thinking of my former teacher and the insanity I'd seen in her eyes. And trust me, I was in a position to know madness.

"Please don't be concerned about her. As far as we can tell, she won't return to this country again. It seems, at this time, that she will remain confined, indefinitely."

The way she talked piqued my curiosity, but before I could even form the thought, Cathryn was shaking her head.

"No, seeing the future is not my gift. You've already guessed what mine is, haven't you? You've had a brush with it. No, I don't know myself, but we have a precog at the

Institute—let's see, maybe you could call her a seer? And we have her check in on various people of interest from time to time, just to make sure everyone is where he should be. Or she should be."

I blinked again. Everything was falling into place—my memories, where I thought I might be—but this girl was the one piece of the puzzle that didn't make sense. *Institute?*

"There's a lot of information we'll give you once you're ready to process it. For now, though, rest." She glanced at the phone in her hand and muttered beneath her breath. "Damn. I've got to go catch a train." She said it as though it were a communicable disease.

"Apparently I need a 'vacation.'" The air quotes were implied by her tone. "At any rate, as I said, you need rest. There are people in place here to make sure everything you need is at your disposal. Your recovery will be rapid, though, and a friend of mine will be here, probably tomorrow, to meet with you. You'll enjoy her. She will be tremendously helpful."

Panic rose in me at the idea that this person, the one connection I had to the real world, was leaving.

She smiled a little and squeezed my hand. "Don't worry. I'll see you again shortly. I don't expect this vacation business to work out, and I promise, as soon as I'm back in Florida, we'll be in touch."

With that she turned and disappeared out the door, leaving me trembling and confused.

CHAPTER
1

IT TURNED OUT THAT being in a coma for over a year was not so great for muscle tone or memory. After the blonde woman left, I must have nodded off for a while, or maybe the rest of the day, and when I opened my eyes again, I panicked.

Where was I?

What happened?

I wanted to jump out of the bed and find someone who could explain, but my legs, heavy on the mattress, had a different plan. I could barely move my arms. When I lifted my hand, hoping to grip the railing and pull myself up to sit, I felt a cool, smooth plastic disc beneath my fingers. It was a button of some sort, and when I clicked it, a disembodied voice floated into the room.

"Hello, Ms. Massler. I'll be with you in a moment."

I turned my head toward the door, which to my utter surprise, stood open. The last place I remembered being was a mental institution, and that place had a strict locked-door policy. As in, I stayed behind the locked doors, and just about everyone else stayed on the other side.

The woman who appeared in the doorway had brown hair pulled back into a braid and smiling blue eyes. She was in her late twenties, I thought, and she wore blue scrubs with daisies on the top. Her white sneakers had soles that let her sneak up on people without a sound.

"Ms. Massler, my name is Casey. I'm so glad to see you awake." She came closer to the bed, without a trace of fear as far as I could detect, and she picked up my wrist, holding it between two of her fingers and thumb. I didn't say anything to distract her while she took my pulse.

"Exactly as it should be." Casey beamed at me as though I were personally responsible for my heart rate being normal. She reminded me a little of a kindergarten teacher.

"Would it be okay if I listened to your heart and took your blood pressure?" Her eyes held mine, and in them I saw a trace of knowledge. She knew who I was, what I'd done, and yet she wasn't afraid. There was compassion there, too. I didn't know what to do with that.

I nodded, still not sure if my voice really worked. With another smile, the nurse unhooked the stethoscope from around her neck, put on the ear pieces and pressed the disc to my chest. She looked off into the distance, listening, and then pulled it away.

"You sound good." She took my blood pressure the same way, with an easy sort of efficiency.

"Ms. Massler, your vitals are all perfect. The doctor will be in later this morning to give you a more thorough examination, but I think she's going to be very happy. Is there anything I can do for you in the meantime?"

I swallowed and managed to point to my throat.

"Water?" I mouthed the word.

Casey slapped a hand to her forehead. "Of course! I'm sorry, that was stupid of me. I'll bring some ice chips in for you now. We'll have to take it slowly until the speech pathologist can come in and do a swallow test, but once you've passed that, you can have anything you want to eat or drink. Hold on, I'll be right back."

She disappeared around the corner, and I closed my eyes. As I adjusted to being awake again, awareness was beginning to creep back into my mind, along with a million questions.

Casey returned with a plastic cup of ice. She held it at the perfect angle for a few to tumble into my mouth. The cold trickled over my tongue and down my throat, washing the bits of my long sleep away with it.

I nodded when I'd had enough, and she set the cup on a table next to my bed. "I'm sure you're going to be tired of hearing this, but rest is the best thing for you right now, until you regain your strength. Like I said, Dr. Simpson will be in shortly, and then Ms. Whitmore told us that someone is coming to visit you this afternoon. If you need anything before then, just hit that call button."

She shot me one more grin before she pivoted and slipped out of the room on her silent shoes. This Casey had to be one of the most incessantly happy people I'd ever seen. Normally, it would have made me want to smack her. But today, I was just happy for the human interaction.

I stared up at the ceiling tiles, going over what I knew so far, trying to remember what the pretty blonde girl had told me. I'd been asleep for a long time, Marica was gone, Tasmyn was safe, and there was some sort of Institute involved in all this.

Florida. She had said that after the vacation that she didn't want to take, she'd be coming back to Florida, which meant that must be where we were now. The last mental hospital I'd been in was in Mississippi. I wondered how I ended back in the Sunshine State. Couldn't have been my father; I knew he wanted me as far away from him as possible.

Thinking about my dad reminded me of my mother, who had been lost to me for so long I could barely picture her face anymore. I had photos, but I knew that they didn't really capture who she was. Sometimes I had glimpses of memories where she was laughing, and I held onto those like precious jewels.

Remembering led to dreaming as I drifted back to sleep. In my mind, I was in our garden with my mother, back in King, in the house that had belonged to her family since the nineteenth century. Gravis King, the town father, had built it for Sarah, my several-times-over-great-grandmother.

We were hidden in the hedges, which meant that no one could see us from the house or from the grounds beyond. I sat on the grass, wearing my favorite ruffled cotton dress in a shade of blue that matched my unusual eyes. In front of me, my mother stood, waving her hands through the air, and as she did, beautiful flowers of every different color danced into being. I clapped my hands in delight, and Mama turned her bright smile on me before she scooped me into her arms.

"Try it, Nell." She dropped to the ground and set me on her crossed legs. "Make the plants grow, baby. You can do it. You have the power."

I couldn't have been more than four, maybe five. I wasn't in school yet. But I scrunched my toddler face together and waited for it to rise: the energy, the magic. Between my mother's tall plants, a bed of clover appeared, topped with fragrant white and purple blossoms.

Mama laughed and plucked one, holding it to her nose to breathe in the fragrance. "Perfect, little one! Doesn't it smell heavenly?" She lowered the bloom to my face, and I mimicked her actions, closing my eyes and inhaling. She laughed all over again.

"My sweet child, look what you've made. This is a gift from our grandmothers, this ability." She ran her hand over the green clover, and it seemed to reach up, trying to touch her. "Don't ever forget what you can do. Don't let anyone take away your wonder in magic."

"I won't, Mama." I smiled up at her, and to my dismay, she began to disappear. I couldn't feel her beneath me, or her hands on my arms. The flowers she'd conjured shriveled and vanished, and my clover turned black. It smelled of death. I struggled to my feet as a dark shadow descended over the hedge, choking me ...

"Ms. Massler—Nell!"

The voice was low but insistent, and I startled awake as the tall woman next to my bed shook my shoulder.

"I'm sorry. I was dreaming." I licked my lips, glancing around for the ice again.

"Here." She held the cup to my lips, and I caught the rim between my teeth, giving me access to the welcome wet coolness.

"Thanks." I shifted on the pillow so that I could see her a little better. She had dark blonde hair, pulled back into neat bun, and large brown eyes that were looking down on me with a mix of concern and curiosity.

"I'm Rebecca Simpson. I've been your doctor for the last seven months. Good to see your eyes open."

"Nice to have them open." My voice was still husky, but my throat didn't feel as dry. I tried to scoot higher in the bed, and to my surprise, I found I had the strength to sit up.

Dr. Simpson was flipping through something on her tablet. "All of your vitals are within normal range, which is excellent. I'll examine you, but I think you'll be ready to begin physical therapy tomorrow."

I did feel stronger, and my mind was clearer, but still, I was surprised. "I've been in a coma for—well, I don't know how long. But someone said it had been a while. Shouldn't I be ... I don't know, taking it slower?"

She smiled a little and perched on the edge of my bed. "You weren't quite in a coma, Ms. Massler. I wasn't your doctor when the incident occurred, of course, but as I understand it, your physical injuries healed completely and should have left no lasting effects. Whatever kept you in that deep, non-responsive sleep—and that's the best term we can use to describe your state, thought it's not entirely accurate—was rooted in something psychological. Or maybe more accurately, something parapsychological."

My mind skirted to that last day with Tasmyn and Marica and then shied away in pain. Nope, wasn't ready to deal with that one yet.

"At any rate, you were in state of suspended animation. Not quite a coma, but more than a natural sleep. I don't have a medical explanation for why you aren't experiencing muscle atrophy. The staff here did work with you daily while you were unconscious, moving your limbs and so on, but still ..." She pursed her lips and shook her head.

"How long exactly was I out? Asleep, or suspended, or whatever you want to call it?"

"Just over a year."

I fell back against the mattress, my breath gone as though I'd been body slammed. *A year?* An entire year of my life, gone? And then I remembered what had passed for my life before that fateful day: a white room, the occasional strait jacket, bland food and no interaction beyond the doctors and nurses assigned to me. If that was what I'd missed, I guessed I couldn't complain. Maybe a long nap wasn't such a bad thing.

"How did I get here? Last thing I knew, I was in a hospital in Mississippi."

Dr. Simpson shrugged. "I don't know, precisely. Dr. Hamilton will be in this afternoon, and you can ask her all those questions. For now, I'm just here to monitor your physical recovery. Is it okay if I take at look at you?"

I nodded, and she went through the normal procedures: listening to my heart, my lungs and my stomach, testing my reflexes and looking at my ears, my eyes and down my throat. She stepped back and began typing into her tablet again, and I straightened my hospital gown.

"Who's Dr. Hamilton?"

"Hmmm?" She frowned, glancing at me over the top of the computer.

"You said Dr. Hamilton was coming in to see me. Who is she?"

"Oh. She's a psychologist from Carruthers. She comes in once a week to monitor your condition."

"I guess she's the one the blonde girl told me about. I'm sorry, I don't remember her name."

"Ms. Whitmore. Yes, that would be it, they're both from Carruthers Initiative Institute." She flipped the stethoscope around her neck and hit a button on her tablet, turning it off. "So you can just rest for now, and then physical therapy will begin tomorrow. If you have any questions, ring for the nurse, and she can always get in touch with me. I'll be back in to check your progress in a few days." She pivoted to leave.

"I have one question now." I spoke up before she could reach the doorway.

"Okay." The doctor didn't come back to my bedside, but she met my eyes.

"When I was in Mississippi, the hospital kept me locked up. I was considered dangerous. But not here. What's the difference? Why the change?"

She raised one shoulder. "I can't answer that. I can only tell you that when I took over your case, I was told that you were no longer a threat." One side of her mouth curled. "Was I misinformed? Do you plan on being a problem?"

I shook my head against the pillow. "No. No problem."

"Excellent. Then I'll see you at the end of the week."

CHAPTER
2

DESPITE DR. SIMPSON'S ASSURANCES that I was going to bounce back faster than most patients, I was still exhausted. I slept again after she left, and when I opened my eyes, I thought I might be dreaming.

The woman who sat in the chair at my bedside was small, with hair that had a base color not too different from my own jet-black curls. But there wasn't much of that color visible: it was covered by just about every other shade I could imagine. Pinks mingled in with greens and blues, and yet somehow it all worked. Her hazel eyes met mine, twinkling.

"I cannot tell you what a pleasure it is to speak with you at last, Nell." She grinned. "We've had some lovely conversations over the past months, but they've been somewhat one-sided."

I stretched my arms, happy to feel the strength in them again. "You must be Dr. Hamilton. I've heard about you."

"All wonderful things, I hope." She offered me her hand. "Would you like to sit up a little more? Have a sip of water?"

I gripped her arm, and a shot of pure energy zinged through my hand, flowing to cover my entire body. A bright orange light flared in front of my eyes. I sucked in a breath, feeling power dance down my fingers and wash over my legs.

"God, what was that?"

Dr. Hamilton laughed. "Just a little pick-me-up, as I like to call it. One of my gifts is energy boosting. Technically, my job is to help you control and refine your abilities, but in a pinch, I can also offer a jolt now and then, something to help you up your game. I've been doing some therapy with you while you were sleeping, and I think it's going to prove to be a big help now."

"Is that why I'm healing so fast?"

"It's part of it, certainly. But you bring your own brand of strength to the table. I have no doubt you'll be completely recovered within a few days, at the latest."

I scooted to sit up. "I want to know what's going on. No one tells me anything, except to wait and ask you. Well, now you're here. I want answers."

If I had expected my tone of voice—no nonsense, take-charge Nell—to rattle this lady, I was sorely disappointed. She smiled again and patted my shoulder. "Of course you do. I know this has to be disconcerting: you fall asleep in a mental health facility in—where was it? Mississippi?—and wake up over a year later in a nursing home in Florida. So ask me anything you want. I promise I'll answer as much as I can. I'll give it to you straight."

I swallowed over the lingering pain in my throat. "What is Carruthers, and what do they want with me?"

"Carruthers Initiative Institute is an organization that exists to bring together those who have extraordinary talents and those who need the help those powers can provide. We serve as facilitators between the two parties."

I frowned. "Extraordinary talents? What do you mean?"

Dr. Hamilton shrugged. "Oh, you can guess at most of them. Mind listeners, precognitives, telekinetics, broadcasters, manipulators, projectors ... the list goes on and on. Anyone who has the ability to do something out of the norm."

My chest tightened a little, and I knew it had nothing to do with any lingering weakness. A group like Carruthers was what I'd been warned about growing up. It was why we never talked about what we could do outside the First Families. Words like 'exploitation' and 'experimentation' ran through my mind. No way I was going to be anyone's lab rat.

"So what does that have to do with me?" I kept my tone casual and curious.

"Nell, you don't have to pretend, and you don't have to be afraid. I promise, we're not here to hurt you, or to use you in any way." Her eye twitched just slightly at that last phrase. "We want to help."

"Why?" It was a valid question. I'd been laying around one hospital or another for the last two and a half years. No one had offered to do anything for me.

"The answer to that is complicated."

I raised my eyebrows, and Dr. Hamilton shook her head.

"No, that's not a cop-out. It's just that I think Cathryn would explain it better. We all have our jobs, and we all have our strong points. My only goal right now is to help you recover. I'd like to learn a little more about what you can do, but we'll figure that out along the way. Cathryn will be back from vacation in a few days, and she'll be happy to explain in more detail. For now, I'd like it if you could trust me." She held up one small hand. "I know you have no reason to do so. I'm a stranger, and in your experience, you can't even depend on your own family, let alone people you don't know. Am I right?"

It was my turn to lift my shoulder and look away, pressing my lips together.

"But could you at least give me a chance? Let's see, how can I convince you ... well, here's something. I know your friend Tasmyn."

I jerked back around. "You know her? How?"

Dr. Hamilton winked at me. "It's sort-of secret, but I'll trust you with the answer. She used to work for Carruthers. I became acquainted with her last fall."

"*Used* to?" I fastened on the key words in that sentence.

"Yes. She still consults for us here and there, but she had a particularly, ah ..." She cast her eyes up as though the word she needed might be on the ceiling. "... troubling case. She's fine, but after that, she decided that she preferred not to work for us full-time."

"But she's okay?" Damn, I hadn't gone to all the trouble of saving her life and almost dying myself just so Tasmyn could run off and die somewhere else.

"Yes, she's perfectly safe. I promise you. Actually, she's been coming up here to see you about once a month or so since the fall."

"Tasmyn visits me?" That was a mind-blower.

"She does. Or she did. She and Michael are back in King for the summer now, but with your permission, I'd like to let

15

her know that you're awake. I think her loyalty has earned her that much."

I nodded. "Sure. That's fine."

"Wonderful." She dropped her hands onto her knees. "Now, let's get down to business. I'd like to talk about what you can do."

"Dr. Hamilton, I really don't--"

"Please call me Zoe. Everyone does, and I prefer it. Dr. Hamilton sounds so stuffy, doesn't it?"

"Zoe. What do you think I can do?"

"Right now, all we have is anecdotal information. I want to hear it from you."

I snorted. "Anecdotal? Just who's been talking to you about me?" I knew for a fact that my family would never say anything. The code of silence was iron-clad and generations old.

"Well, Tasmyn, mostly. And ... your father."

"My father told you I had some kind of power?" My heart thumped. Daddy dearest had loose lips these days, apparently.

Zoe ignored my question. "From what I can tell, it seems you have some telekinesis and perhaps some projection. And maybe a few other goodies I haven't verified. Can you transfer matter?"

"Transfer—no. What do you mean?"

"Move objects through space. Years ago, at a carnival, for instance, people might have thought those objects were disappearing when they saw magicians perform the trick."

I didn't answer her.

"Those are the gifts I'm pretty sure about. But one has me curious. I've heard you can cast fire. Care to comment?"

I let my head fall back against the mattress. "I don't know what you want me to say. This is insane. Is it some kind of test?"

"No, Nell, it's not a test. We're only here looking out for your best interest. Now, you can choose not to talk with me, and in that case, you'll stay in that bed until the doctors decide you're ready to be released, at which point you'll be on your own. You'll have freedom, complete and unencumbered. And you'll be alone."

Alone. Again. It wasn't a new concept. I'd been by myself in one form or another since I was six. But for whatever reason, the idea hit me hard in this moment.

"Or you can trust me. And if you do, and decide you like what we have to offer at the Institute, you'll have a job, and a family who will support you, no matter what. Carruthers is a business. But we're also family, which I know sounds cliché, but in this case, it's also the truth. Cathryn's great-great-grandfather established the company, and since then, it's been a family affair. All of us who work there are ... different. The rest of the world doesn't see things the way we do. When you're part of the Institute, you're surrounded by others who understand the challenges you face. It's not something I take lightly, and given your history, I doubt you would, either."

I closed my eyes. She was setting a choice before me, I understood that. Three years ago, I would have ... well, I didn't know. In those days I was hungry for the power, wanting more, and needing to understand what I could do and where it had come from. I might have jumped at the chance to be with people who could give me that. But right now, having some place to go where I wouldn't be alone was even more appealing.

"Okay." I finally opened my eyes. "I'll try. I can't promise anything. I'm not a people person. I don't play well with others. But I'll give it a shot."

"That's all we ask." Zoe sat back in her chair. "Now, let's talk about you."

It was hard, sharing about myself. I licked my lips. "I can move things with my mind. Telekinesis, right? And I can ... well, I'd just begun to learn to make things disappear. You're right, they didn't really vanish, but I could send them away."

"Like the athame you moved the night you were in the clearing in King, ready to kill Amber?" She spoke so casually, but still, I flinched.

"I'm glad to see you don't hold back." I tucked the edge of the white sheet beneath my hip. "Yes, I sent the athame to my room at home."

"Mmmhmm. What about the fire?"

"I can cast fire. Marica taught me."

"Ah." Zoe pursed her lips. "Very interesting. Did you know that fire casting and fire starting are not the same? The power comes from a different place. Casting is deliberate, a learned ability. Starting is ... instinctive. Both usually originate in emotion, but while fire casting tends to be passionate, fire starters often use it defensively, when they feel powerless or afraid."

I met her gaze. "I'm not afraid of anything. What I do with fire is always on purpose."

Zoe nodded. "Understood. Now, the projecting. According to Tasmyn, you visited her in dreams several times over the months between your commitment to the hospital and the day you fell asleep. How did you do that?"

I spread my fingers over the blanket. "I had been experimenting before ... when I was still in King. I hadn't gotten very far, though. When I was in the hospital, I wanted to know what was happening. At first, it was—well, I wanted revenge for what Tasmyn did, replacing me in Marica's eyes and putting me into the psych ward. Then the longer I thought about it, I realized that Marica had used me. Tasmyn wasn't really my enemy."

"That was must have been quite a revelation."

"It was. In King, I had read that projecting through dreams was the best way to begin. The only requirements were some crystals and a shared setting. Of course, it wasn't really a dream, so much as it was a subconscious visitation. The guards we keep around our minds naturally drop during sleep, so if I could focus on a place where we'd both been, I could project my own subconscious there and engage whoever it was I wanted to see."

Zoe tilted her head. "Why were you trying to project at that point, Nell? Before you were in the hospital."

I glanced away. "My mother. I thought maybe I could try to contact her. But I didn't get far enough before ... well, before."

"Ah. And then once you were in the hospital, you decided to use the same techniques?"

"As far as I could. I didn't have crystals, of course, but I had read that a substitute was possible."

"What was that?"

She already knew the answer. I could hear it in her voice. But I guessed she needed to hear it from me.

"Blood."

"And you had plenty of that at hand."

I laughed, a sharp bark that sounded rusty from disuse. "Yes, you could say that. I didn't need much. It wasn't hard to get hold of a piece of metal and sharpen it, and as long as I kept the cuts hidden under my clothes, no one was noticed. The first time was the hardest, because they caught me at it. I made my blade disappear, but the doctors put me into a strait jacket. I brought the knife back into my hand, maneuvered it to skin, and I was in business."

"You went to a lot of trouble for a visit. What did you get out of it?"

I lay back again, sinking into the pillows. The walk down memory lane was draining me.

"I talked to Tasmyn. I made it a point to keep my eye on her. I could almost read her mind when I was projecting, so I knew what she was feeling and planning to do. It gave me something to think about other than myself."

"You tried to keep her from getting too involved with Marica."

"I tried. But Marica could be persuasive. It's not surprising Tasmyn didn't listen to me. The temptation was too great." I struggled to keep my eyes open.

Zoe stretched her arms in front of her and yawned. "I'm feeling your fatigue, Nell. As you might have guessed, I have empathic tendencies. You need some more rest, but I'll be back tomorrow, and we'll get to work."

I wriggled myself flat and echoed the doctor's yawn. "Okay. What kind of work?"

She stood and laid her hand on the top of my head, just briefly. I didn't feel the same jolt that I had earlier; instead, a wave of well-being and relaxation swept down my body.

"Exercising your abilities. It's time to reclaim your power."

CHAPTER 3

"NO, NO, NO—WATCH the window!"

Zoe ducked as the blue orb narrowly missed the top of her head and careened off the thin strip of wall between two sets of windows. It landed on the tile floor and splintered.

"Sorry." I leaned against the bed. I'd been awake for four days now, and most of the time I felt completely normal. But every once in a while, fatigue crept up on me. Zoe assured me that it was normal, but I was impatient with myself. Not only did I still need a nap, but my telekinesis left something to be desired, too.

"Not your fault." She pulled a few stiff paper towels from the wall dispenser and knelt to brush up the pieces of glass. "You're doing much better. And your power is expanding. I should have realized that we would need a bigger space."

"I could barely keep the orb from crashing through the window. I don't look at that as progress. I want to be better, now. Not in a week."

The glass tinkled against the trash can as Zoe dumped

it. "You're working hard. Have a little patience with your-self." She looked over my shoulder, tilting her head as she was listening to a voice I couldn't hear.

"Why don't we try a change of scenery? Let's go out-side and practice some new tricks."

My eyes widened. "I can go outside?"

She shrugged, smiling. "Of course you can. Why not?"

"Zoe, strait jackets and padded walls. Those were my life before I went into the coma. Letting me have the run of the place feels weird."

"Well, those days are over. At least, they are if you choose for them to be." She shot me what I'd come to think of as a patented-Zoe-expression, full of encouragement and earnest belief. "The decision is yours. It always has been."

She was talking about more than just confinement. I felt the weight of her words; how many times had I made the bad choice? Taken the wrong road. Somehow I had a second chance now, and I couldn't help feeling I didn't deserve it.

"Outside sounds good." I thrust my feet into the stand-ard hospital issue slippers, and Zoe handed me my robe. I was beginning to hate the thing.

"Zoe, do you think I could start wearing real clothes soon? I'm so over this stuff." I gestured down my body. "I'm dreaming of jeans and t-shirts."

"Sure. I'll bring you some tomorrow. I should have thought of that, I'm sorry. So much on my mind right now." She swung open the door and gestured for me to go ahead of her into the hallway. My heart pounded a little; I hadn't been outside of this room since I'd been transferred, and I hadn't walked through any door without some kind of restraint in a long time.

I followed Zoe toward what must have been the nurses' station, where a few people looked up and smiled. I half-expected one of them to run and sound an alarm, but no one did. We turned the corner and headed for a set of double doors that led outside.

The sunshine hit my face, and instinctively, I turned toward it, breathing in the heat. A breeze teased my hair, blowing it across my nose, but I didn't move. This was a moment I couldn't rush.

Zoe must have sensed as much, because she didn't speak until I opened my eyes and took a step forward.

"Thank you." Emotion was not something I did, ever, and I couldn't remember the last time I had been grateful for anything. But right now, just the act of being outside overwhelmed me with a sense of something I couldn't quite name.

Zoe didn't question my statement. She patted my arm and moved further into the courtyard. "You're welcome. Come this way. There's a little section that is shielded from all the windows, and we can be private there."

A small picnic table sat in the middle of the grass, and I sat down across from Zoe. I noticed she was absently fingering her necklace, and I frowned, remembering her earlier words.

"Are you okay, Zoe? You said you have something on your mind."

She smiled and covered my hand with hers. "Nell, you amaze me. For a girl who apparently has difficulty thinking of others or empathizing, you just thanked me and expressed concern."

A flush of pleasure spread over my face. I had forgotten

what it was like to be praised. It felt ... odd.

"Is there something wrong with me, that I can't do that like other people?" It was a question I'd wrestled with for a long time in the hospital, before the coma.

Zoe shook her head. "Not at all. Your emotional maturity took a hit in early childhood, and you've been struggling with that since." She sat back and rested her chin in her hands. "But like everything else, it's a choice. If you choose to consider others, pretty soon it will become natural. An ingrained part of your being."

I wasn't sure I wanted that. Pain lay in that direction, I was fairly sure. But I couldn't help myself from asking the question again.

"But are you all right?"

"I'm worried, Nell, and I'm grieving. We learned recently that we lost one of our team. She was killed while undercover. I was particularly close to this girl, and my heart is broken. You can understand that."

I nodded, frowning. "Who killed her?"

"We don't know details. It's long and complicated, and Cathryn will explain when she gets home."

"You said you're worried. Why? Because other people are in danger?"

Zoe sighed. "Yes, one in particular who was on the assignment with her. And more than that, what happened up there calls into question what we do and the safety of ..." Her voice trailed off, and she cut her eyes to me. "I'm sorry, Nell. There's no need for you to be worried. That's just my overactive imagination."

I lifted one shoulder. "It doesn't frighten me. I told you, nothing does. I'm not going to bail on Carruthers just because there might be danger."

Zoe grinned and stood up. "Good girl. Now let's try some earth work. Want to grow some plants?"

I winced just a little, remembering my dream from earlier in the week. "I'll try. I haven't done that in a long time. It was the first thing my mother taught me." The words tumbled out without me thinking about them. I never talked about my mother, and I certainly didn't discuss what she had taught me. Something about Zoe encouraged sharing. I was going to have to be wary around her.

"Grow something over there." She pointed to a spot of grass about four feet away, and I squinted at it. Taking a deep breath, I sent out the gentle encouragement I remembered ... found what I needed ... and coaxed it into coming forth, bleeding small bits of energy in the direction of the plants. Nothing too strong that might destroy the tender greens, but enough to accelerate the natural growth cycle.

Within moments, shoots appeared above the grass line, and a few seconds later, fragrant purple-tipped white blossoms topped the stalks.

"Pretty." Zoe leaned over and sniffed. "And they smell so sweet. Clover, hmm? I would have expected something more dramatic from you, I think."

I kept my eyes fastened on the ring of flowers. "I'm over drama. Simplicity feels right."

Zoe laid her hand on my shoulder. "I understand. Well, you haven't lost your knack with earth energy, though I'd like to see what else you can do with it once we're back at Harper Creek."

I had learned over the past few days that Carruthers was headquartered in an antebellum estate a few hours away from the hospital. Zoe referenced it casually, without any doubt that I'd be going there with her.

"When do you think that will be?" I rubbed my knee through the thin cotton of my hospital gown.

"Cathryn is scheduled to be back in two days. Once she comes to the hospital and talks with you, we can probably have you at the Institute within a day or two."

I cocked my head. "Assuming the doctors agree, right?"

The side of Zoe's mouth turned up. "Of course. But that won't be a problem." She ran one hand through her multi-colored hair. "Now, I wonder if we could talk about something ... less pleasant. Normally I wouldn't do bring it up so soon, but in this case, time is of the essence. We can't wait, I'm afraid."

I drew my brows together. Why were we in a time crunch? Before I could ask, Zoe continued.

"You told me about transporting to see Tasmyn in her dreams. Or rather meeting on a level of her subconscious, which is probably a more accurate term. But we haven't discussed your final visit to King. The day you saved Tasmyn's life."

I flinched. I didn't have good memories of that day, but then again, how was it different from any other day of my existence? Distracting Marica had given Tasmyn enough time to get away, and the cost to my own life had been worth that. Hadn't it?

"What do you want to know?" I kept my voice neutral, non-committal.

"How did you do it? Tasmyn wasn't asleep, and clearly Marica could see you, too. And how did you know that Tasmyn was in danger?"

So many questions. I closed my eyes, letting the memory wash over me. "I found out after my first few visits to Tasmyn that we maintained some sort of connection even after I'd left her mind. I guess it was one-way, since she didn't seem to know anything about what *I* was thinking or feeling. I could sense her emotions, especially if they were very strong, and I could feel the power. It was like getting a fix every time she used her abilities. I got this hit ... and I could also feel who was around her. Well, not all the time. But if it were Marcia or that Brooks boy, everything was heightened. She thrummed a little higher, and I could even get glimpses sometimes of what she was seeing."

Zoe tapped her finger on her cheek. "Fascinating. I've never heard of anything quite like that. And Tasmyn never mentioned the connection to me, either, so I think we're safe to assume she didn't feel it. Is it still there? Can you sense her?"

I shook my head. "No. Almost as soon as I woke up I wondered if I could feel her, but it was gone."

"It's likely that your visits were necessary to maintain that line."

"Maybe." I stared down at the grass, remembering. "Anyway, that day, I woke up not planning to do anything more than annoy the nurses and stare at the ceiling. Then that afternoon, I felt a blast of power. It was insane. I almost—" I flushed, thinking of that sensation. "It's a very intimate feeling, sharing that power. I wanted to just lie there and enjoy it. But I could feel Tasmyn's panic, her worry, and I knew it was connected to whatever she had done. I didn't know what had happened, but as the day went on, I felt her fear. And then a kind of peace. I knew she ended things with the boy, but she was ramping up for something else, to cut her ties with Marica. I figured that wasn't going to be easy, so I decided to do whatever I had to do, to keep her ... safe."

Zoe laid her hand on my arm and rubbed it lightly. "And just what did that involve?"

I smiled, my lips tight over my teeth. "Blood, and lots of it. Mine. The magic's in the blood, you know, and I needed a big push to get me to King outside a dream share. I cut deeper and in more places, and there I was, in Marica's house. She was crazy. I mean, seriously, bat-shit crazy. She was holding the athame to Tasmyn's throat. Talk about déjà vu ..."

I saw it in my mind again. Marica's house, with the table full of crystals and knives and other accoutrements belonging to her family ... the familiar girl in the chair, her hands gripping the seat as Marica crooned chilling words and threatened her with the ceremonial knife. Tasmyn's face when she spotted me across the room.

Amazing the lengths I'll go just to say I told you so, Tasmyn.

"I knew Tas could handle getting away if I could distract Marica. So I did. And she ran. She used the water as a defense, and once she was gone, Marica came at me with the athame. Ironic, right? The last thing I saw was that knife about to plunge into me. And then it was dark."

I put my hand to my face and was amazed to feel wetness. I never cried. Never. I took a deep breath and stiffened my back.

"The next thing I remember is Cathryn calling my name. That's all."

"Thank you, Nell." Zoe squeezed my arm. "I know that

wasn't easy, but it helps."

"I can't do it again." If this was why they wanted me, Carruthers was sore out of luck. No more. I was done with risking my life for magic. Now I only wanted peace. "I'm not afraid of it, but unless it's life or death, no way."

Zoe's eyes narrowed. "What if it is life or death? And what if you could do it without blood? I mean, without shedding blood."

"Whose life?"

She slid her gaze away from mine. "I can't say, not yet. But trust me, Nell. We would never force you to risk your life, not even to save someone else."

I shivered, and Zoe stood up.

"Come on. The sun is going down. Enough for today."

CHAPTER 4

MY FIRST IMPRESSION OF CATHRYN Whitmore had been a little fuzzy, being that I was just coming out of a coma. But I was wide-awake when I saw her the next time, and the sense of her power hit me hard.

Cathryn was smaller than I had expected. She was slender, and her blonde hair was as white as I remembered. It fell around her shoulders in a cascade this time, instead of being away from her face. Her face seemed softer, too, but maybe that was just my imagination, since I had been barely lucid when we'd first met.

"Nell, you look wonderful." She smiled at me, and there was more warmth there than I expected. I had been thinking of her as an ice queen these last few days, though I didn't know why. Again, maybe just a mistaken impression.

"Thank you. I feel better than I did when you ... before you left."

"Excellent. Zoe tells me you've been making amazing progress. It sounds like you're nearly ready to come home."

Home. And where exactly was that?

Cathryn pulled up a chair and sat down next to my bed, where I perched cross-legged. Zoe had come through with the real-people clothes, so I had on a pair of the softest jeans I'd ever worn and an oversized green tee. Leaving behind the hospital gowns made me feel almost normal.

"I realize you have a lot of questions. I'm going to remind you that I can hear what you're thinking if you don't keep your mind guarded. Do you know how to do that?"

I remembered Marica's lessons on that topic, something she had ramped up considerably after Tasmyn had arrived in King. "Sort of. Marica taught me, so I think I can do it."

"Okay. We'll help you learn how to keep a more effective block up once we're back at the Institute. It's essential with all the people there who have abilities. Of course, it's for your protection and theirs, too. But for now, please forgive me if I accidentally answer a question that you haven't asked. When I'm deep in a conversation, sometimes that happens."

"No problem." I shifted on the bed. "Zoe told me a little about Carruthers, and that you want me to come work for you. I think I get that. But I want to know how I woke up, and why now? Did you do that? Bring me back? And what do you expect of me?"

"All valid concerns. I'll give you the answers that I can. First, we didn't exactly wake you up. I merely tipped the cart. Zoe has been visiting you weekly for months, as I think she told you, and she's been able to accelerate your healing and restore you. I think you would have opened your eyes on your own pretty soon anyway, but we didn't know for certain. Which leads me to the why now."

She took a deep breath and stared at the tile floor for a

moment. "We have a situation, and it's bad. One of our people—"

"Died. I know. Zoe told me. And the other one is in danger, right? That's why you need me. You woke me up for a mission." My hands fisted on my knees. I couldn't fall into the trap of thinking someone really wanted me just for myself. I was a tool, a means to an end. Why should these two women be any different?

"I'm not going to lie to you, Nell. We do need you. But when we ..." She trailed off, and her eyes flickered. I sensed she was going to say something but had thought better of it. "We don't have plans to use you. You're not a tool."

I gritted my teeth. That fast I had forgotten this chick could hear my thoughts. I had to be more careful.

"I will never use what you think against you, Nell. I'm sorry I heard that. The truth is, yes, we accelerated your awakening because we hope you can help save a life. Probably more than one. But even if you decide you don't want to be part of this mission, we still want you. We will help you, no matter what. You're valuable to us for who you are, not for what you can do."

I swallowed hard. I had fallen for a line before. I could hear echoes of Marica's words. *Nell, you are my daughter. This was meant to be. I will never treat you like your family did. Together we can turn the world upside down ...*

"I'm not Marica Lacusta." Cathryn's voice was sharper. "God, I'm tired of you and Tasmyn and the damage that woman did to you. Please, Nell. I know you have trust issues. But I'm being honest with you. Let me explain everything before you start thinking of all the ways I might be trying to take advantage of you."

I nodded. "Okay. I'll try to keep my mind open." A smile lifted one side of my lips. "I mean, I'll listen. I guess all minds are open to you."

"Pretty much." Cathryn smiled, too. "All right, Nell, I'm not going to play games. This is the situation. Last fall, we recruited someone from one of the First Families of King. You don't know him personally, but from what Zoe has told me, you know of him, through Tasmyn. Rafe Brooks is a manipulator, and he became part of Carruthers."

The Brooks boy. I remembered Tasmyn's conflicted feelings about him, the pull he had on her heart and mind, and the temptation he had offered. He hated Marica, I knew that. But Tas had walked away from him right before she escaped the Romanian witch's clutches. I wondered how he had gotten over that.

"Rafe and Jocelyn—Jocelyn Pennell, his recruiter—went on an undercover mission together. A series of events indicated that something was going on at what appeared to be a commune in southern Georgia. We learned that there was a connection to a company that manufactures weapons, and to a young woman who can apparently kill with her mind. She took out one of our clients, which was what led to our involvement and to the assignment for Rafe and Jocelyn." Cathryn's blue eyes clouded and grew distant as she remembered.

"There's more to the story, and I'll fill you in later. You know Tasmyn worked for us for a time, and she was involved in a job that was part of this whole web. But what's important for you to know now is that while Jocelyn and Rafe were in Georgia, something went wrong. We're not certain of details, but we know that Joss was killed, probably by that same girl. Her name is Mallory Jones, and we don't know anything about her, other than that she has this ability, and she's connected to whatever is happening in Georgia."

"How do you know what happened at the commune?" I was trying to follow along, but there was so much information, I was having a hard time keeping it all straight.

Cathryn massaged her temple with two fingers. I could almost feel the pain in her head. "We have a precog at Carruthers. Fiona had been keeping an eye on the situation for us, but as you might know, precognition is far from being an exact science. Everything in the world is in flux at all times, and the future is seldom set in stone. We think, from what she saw that day, that Jocelyn's murder was not premeditated. From what we can piece together, it seems Ms. Jones made an unexpected appearance at the camp and recognized Rafe and Jocelyn from their previous encounter in New Orleans, where our client died. We think they tried to get away, and in that attempt, Jocelyn died."

I felt an unfamiliar stab of regret for the loss of a girl I had never met, had never even heard of until Zoe had mentioned her the other day.

"What happened to Rafe?" I licked my lips and focused on keeping up the guard in my mind. I didn't want my feelings to make me more vulnerable to Cathryn.

"He was hurt, we know that. And we're almost positive they're keeping him prisoner there, at the camp. As soon as we could, we sent in another operative to try to rescue him. We didn't hear from him for weeks, and then Fiona finally picked up his path again. He was in a hospital in Savannah, badly beaten. Barely alive. We brought him back to Florida as soon as we could, but he had no memory of anything after arriving at the camp. He can't tell us if Rafe is still alive ... though Fiona is certain of it. But she also feels he doesn't have long."

The room spun a little around me, and I grabbed the edge of the bed. "Why does she think that?"

Cathryn blew out a sigh. "Fiona can sense intent, and she believes the people at the camp are getting ready for something big. Part of that may include getting rid of Rafe."

I nodded. I hadn't known a precog before, but I couldn't imagine the sense of frustration ... of being able to see what might happen, but being powerless to stop it or to change it. And that would extend to Cathryn and Zoe, and everyone else at Carruthers, too.

"Exactly." Cathryn folded her hands on her lap, but her fingers were tight, gripping together. "So while I'm telling you the truth when I say we didn't wake you up to use you, I'll admit that we pushed the issue, moved you along a little faster, because we need your ability. We need what you can do."

"Which is what?" My powers flitted across my mind's eye, but I knew what she meant. Someone who could transport across space, who could project, would be an invaluable asset to this company, particularly right now.

"Yes." Cathryn leaned forward. "Nell, you are the most powerful person I've ever met, and I've been in this business my whole life. My family has gifts, and we've been working with extraordinary people as long as I can remember—well, longer than that. But you're beyond anyone I've known. I think you could be the key to saving Rafe, and maybe even bringing down this whole network of ... evil."

"Evil?" I raised one eyebrow.

"I might be overstating it, but I don't think so. Carruthers has been linking people who have gifts with those who need them for generations, and we've never come across such organized plans for out-and-out terror. We only have glimpses of what they plan to do, but what we're learning terrifies me, frankly. It's on a scope beyond what we guessed in the beginning."

If Cathryn were trying to entice me with pretty promises, I might have been put off. But the idea of fighting evil— if that was really what was going on—that was tempting. What did I have to lose?

"Okay." I swung my legs over the side of the bed and faced Cathryn.

"Okay, what?" She met my eyes with a frown.

"Okay, I'm in. I want to be part of this fight. I'll help you save Rafe. Just tell me what you need me to do."

"Just like that?"

I shrugged. "I want peace. I want to be left alone. That's all true. But I have some amends to make. Some atonement, I guess." A long-ago dream conversation with Tasmyn echoed in my head.

"... *maybe I'll know a little redemption too. I guess redemption is painful after all.*"

The scars on my arms and neck throbbed a little, but it was a hurt I welcomed. It meant I was alive, and that I had a second chance, after all.

Now that I knew what I had to do, had an idea of the

plan, I was anxious to get started. Two days after Cathryn's return, I stood in the center of my hospital room, glancing around, waiting for her to arrive and take me to Harper Creek. I tapped my foot with impatience and then grinned at the red sneaker making the noise. It had been so long since I'd been able to wear real shoes. Even though I'd never been a jeans-and-sneaker kind of girl, at this point I loved anything that wasn't hospital cotton.

"Ready to leave us, Ms. Massler?" A woman I had only seen in passing pushed open my door and leaned in. She wore a light gray suit with black pumps, and her smile was genuine. Her name tag said she was Leah from the accounting department.

"Yes. No offense, but if I don't see the inside of a hospital for the rest of my life, it's okay with me."

Leah laughed and came inside, shaking her head. "I can completely understand that. And don't worry, I'm not offended. Most of our patients feel the same way. Though of course, few actually do walk out of here, since this is long-term care. But we like our success stories." She handed me a clipboard that held a pile of papers. "I just need a few signatures, if you don't mind."

"Um, sure." For the first time, it occurred to me that I didn't know anything about the details of my hospital stay. Did my father's insurance cover it? Was I going to have to pay for them hosting me during my year-and-a-half long nap?

"It's just legal stuff, making sure all the T's are crossed and the I's dotted. Everything is taken of financially. No worries."

"Ah, okay." I took the papers and began signing where

she pointed out the X's. I skimmed the lines, taking in the legal mumbo-jumbo until one sentence caught my eye.

"What does this mean?" I pointed to the paper, and the accountant leaned over my shoulder to look.

"Oh, that's just indicating who is financially responsible for you and for your stay here. Nothing to worry about."

"It says Carruthers Initiative Institute."

"Yes, that's right. The Institute is handling your bills."

"Why?" I looked up at her, frowning. "Why isn't my father paying for this?"

"Hmmm ..." Leah bit her lip and flipped through the papers. "I don't really know. I've only worked here for three months, and that whole time, we've billed Carruthers. I just assumed—well, you know. That you worked for them."

I nodded slowly and signed the last few lines. Leah took the clipboard back from me, a wrinkle between her eyes as she glanced at me.

"You should ask Ms. Whitmore about the billing and your father. She's always been my contact at Carruthers. I'm sure she can explain."

"Yeah, thanks." I watched as Leah left the room, her heels clicking as though she couldn't get out of there fast enough. I sat down on the bed and smoothed a wrinkle on the sheet.

"Well, are you ready to blow this pop stand?" Cathryn breezed in, impeccable as always. Her hair was back in its twist, but her smile was warm.

"I really am. But I need to ask you something first."

"Certainly." Cathryn tilted her head, looking at me with expectation.

"Why is Carruthers listed as the responsible party on my

release papers? Why isn't my father paying for me?"

Cathryn sucked in a deep breath and sighed. "I'm sorry about that, Nell. I wasn't trying to hide anything from you, but I didn't realize this would come up so soon. Your father turned over full custody of you and your financial affairs to Carruthers last fall. We've been making all the medical decisions regarding your care since then."

I thought I was beyond the point of being surprised or hurt by anything Nick Massler could do, but I was wrong. The floor beneath me felt as though it slanted.

"Why? I mean, I get we weren't close. He wasn't father-of-the-year, and I wasn't exactly a doting daughter. But ... I never thought he would just wash his hands of me."

"It was a little more involved than that, and part of it was my fault." Cathryn sat next to me on the bed and laced her hands together loosely. She didn't look at me as she spoke.

"Remember I told you that Tasmyn had worked for us last year? And there was a case that had been connected to the weapons ring we suspect is running out of the commune in Georgia?"

I nodded, dreading where this might be going. Was my father part of this plot? I always thought he was just an inconsiderate bastard. I never suspected him of being capable of anything truly heinous.

"In that case, your father was our client. His, ahh ..." She rolled her eyes to the ceiling. "The girl he was seeing was murdered, and your father was a suspect. He hired us to prove his innocence. Nick thought an old friend who's now a political rival had killed the girl to frame him, ruin his chances in the senate race."

"He was going to run for office?" I shook my head. "I guess once he got the crazy wife and daughter put away, it was all going to be smooth sailing. Nice."

Cathryn went on as though I hadn't spoken. "Tasmyn went to work for Congressman Remington—that was the rival. She volunteered as part of his campaign to try to figure out whether he was guilty. To make a long and sordid story short, Remington's campaign manager was ... well, we're not sure what or who he was. But he was manipulating the situation and had arranged the girlfriend's murder. He and one of our agents, who was working against us, both disappeared. We assume they're dead, but no bodies were found."

"God." I shook my head. "Turns out you miss a lot when you're in a coma for over a year. But Tasmyn was okay, right?"

"Yes." Cathryn leaned back a little on the bed, propping herself on one arm. "She did quite well for herself, protected her own life and that of the congressman. She also gave your father a lecture about his treatment of you, or so I heard." There was just a hint of amusement in her voice.

"Good for her." I shifted so that I could see Cathryn better. "That's all very interesting, but it doesn't explain why my father decided to disown me."

"That's not entirely accurate. And like I said, it is probably more my fault. When Nick came to us, to ask for help, he said he'd pay any amount if we could clear his name. We did charge him, but I also added my own request. I stipulated that he turn your care over to us in return for our work."

"Why on earth would you do that?" My throat tightened. Had my first instinct been right, that Carruthers only wanted me to experiment with my powers?

"No, Nell. That's not true. To be honest, my father was against me making the request. He feels strongly about family, and he was afraid you'd react just as you are. I had to fight him and the other members of the Carruthers board of directors. But I won." She smiled and closed her eyes. "I almost always win. But this time, it meant more."

A shiver danced down my spine, and I pulled up my mind blocks. Why did Cathryn want me?

"Even before Tasmyn gave Nick hell, I had met your father. He's not so good at the blocking, you know, and I got a good sense of who he is. And we'd been following your story, since we monitor most of the First Families in King. I knew what had happened to you, that you were here at St. Bruno's by this time. I thought maybe we could help you, but we couldn't do it unless we had full access to you and to your medical records."

"And my father, I'm sure, was just distraught at the idea of handing over responsibility for his freak daughter. I bet he cried big old crocodile tears." It hurt. I hated him, I had hated him for years, but damn it, this still hurt.

"He was surprised. He asked me what we intended to do with you. I told you the truth: that you have tremendous potential, but that up to now, you hadn't been in the right environment to cultivate your abilities. For good use." Cathryn shot me a meaningful look. "I said that we had the experience to help you. I said that he would be making the most selfless choice by allowing us to take over."

"I still don't really get why you did it. I'm not anything special, Cathryn. I'm fucked up. Excuse my language, but it's the truth. I'm wrong. Everything I touch goes bad and dies. I know you want to do the right thing here, but your best option would be to just let me go. I'll live by myself, away from people. I won't hurt anyone."

"Nell, you're being ridiculous." The softness in Cathryn's voice undercut her crisp words. "You're not going away by yourself. And I fought for you because I hate to see waste of any kind." She crossed her ankles and stared down at her hands. "I grew up with a loving family. My father doesn't have any special abilities, but he married into a family full of them, and he accepted me without any reservation. From birth, I was surrounded by people who celebrated my gifts, and after some of the stories I've heard from our people, I know just how rare that is. I hate that your father couldn't see what a treasure he had in you. I'm sorry about your mother, and I'm sorry you had to grow up so much on your own. But that part of your life is over, and now, if you'll only accept it, you can have a new family, full of people who will love you the way you are."

I rolled my eyes. "That's the biggest bunch of sentimental bullshit I've ever heard. I don't need people to love me. That only leads to more pain. And I've had plenty of that to last two lifetimes, thanks very much."

To my surprise, Cathryn laughed. "Okay, Nell. Whatever you say. If you don't want love, how about respect? How about the chance to help others and earn the admiration of your co-workers? Or earn a little of that redemption you mentioned the other day?"

I looked out through the window at the sunshine dancing over the tree branches, and I thought about Cathryn's words. I pictured the Brooks boy, prisoner in some camp in Georgia, needing rescue. Could I walk away now, knowing I might have helped?

"I'll try," I said finally. "That's all I can do."

"And that's all we ask of you." Cathryn stood, as though she wanted to pull me out before I changed my mind again. "Now come on. It's time for you to come home."

CHAPTER
5

THE HOUSE I GREW up in was the largest and grandest in King. It had been the first house built in town, and it was designed and paid for by Gravis King himself, the founder of our quirky little community. The grounds covered several acres and included a massive lawn and several separate gardens. It was rumored to contain one of the most powerful mystical epicenters within King.

So I didn't expect to be impressed by Harper Creek as Cathryn and I turned down the road toward the house. When we rounded the first corner and the large white house came into view, though, my mouth dropped open a little.

"This is home." Cathryn slid me a sideways glance, with a smirk. "I hope you'll feel that way, too. Harper Creek is headquarters for Carruthers, but it's also my family's center. My great-great-great-grandfather built this house, and it's been ours for well over a century."

Her baby blue Thunderbird purred up the driveway and around the corner of the house, into a small parking lot in the back. She pulled away from the other cars, parking in a corner that seemed designed for her car.

"No one gets near my baby." She grinned at me as we opened our doors. "My whole family is a little car-crazy, so I hope you'll understand when I say, keep your hands off."

I laughed, a sound that felt rusty from disuse. "Don't worry about me. I'm not a car person. I can't tell a Ford from a Fiat."

Cathryn shook her head in mock horror. "That's terrible. We'll convert you yet. Come on, Zoe's waiting for us."

The door on the back of the house was nearly hidden by green bushes. I followed Cathryn as she opened it and stepped into a kitchen. A huge man with a puff of gray hair stood in front of the stove, flipping something in a pan.

"Henry, this is Nell. She's going to be here with us for a while. Nell, Henry keeps all of us fed and happy here at Harper Creek."

"Miss Nell." He bowed deeply, holding the spatula out in his arm. "I'm happy to meet you. And please feel free to come down and cook any time. My kitchen is your kitchen."

I forced a smile. "Thanks, but cooking and me ..." I shook my head. "Bad stuff. I can't do it."

Henry grinned. "Even better, because nobody heats up my kitchen like I do. So you just tell me what you like to eat, and I'll make sure you get it."

I shrugged. "I'm not picky. I guess I'm not much of an eater, either."

Henry reached to turn a knob on the stove. "I look at that as a personal challenge. Is there anything you don't like? Can't eat?"

I tilted my head, thinking. "No, I don't think so. I usually just eat whatever is in front of me."

"She's been eating hospital food for the last few years, Henry. I think whatever you make is going to be a vast improvement over that." Cathryn moved to the doorway. "If you'll excuse us, Zoe's waiting upstairs."

I smiled over my shoulder at the chef and followed Cathryn down a hall and up a small set of stairs. It was quiet, but I could feel others around us ... people with power. I had nearly forgotten what that felt like, to be in a home where every person had some sort of gift. Like most members of the First Families in King, I could sense abilities; it was second nature for me.

The house itself breathed history and presence. I trailed one finger along the dark wood banister, as a memory flashed across my mind.

I was standing in the living room, surrounded by highly polished wood and huge portraits. An old woman—my Gammy, who died when I was only five—sat behind me on the overstuffed velvet sofa.

"This is your legacy, Nell darling. This house, and all who lived in it, from Great-great-grandmother Sarah, on down through me, and your mother, and now you. Can you feel them?"

I nodded, my eyes wide.

"Never forget, my love. Your name may be Massler, but you are a Vrajitoare. Make your ancestors proud. Live your legacy ..."

"Nell, are you with me?" Cathryn stood at the top of the stairs, while I had frozen three steps down.

"Yeah." I moved toward her. "Sorry. It just ... reminded me of something. Being here. Feeling all the power around me. Weird."

"Don't be afraid of your memories. At least, that's what Zoe always says."

"And I'm always right." Her vibrant head poked out of a room behind Cathryn. "Come on, we have so much to do, and never enough time."

She disappeared again, and Cathryn waved me forward to join them in what looked like a conference room. We sat down at a long table.

"What do we have to do?" I glanced from one of them to the other. "I thought maybe I'd have a little time to settle in. Rest."

"Don't you feel well?" Cathryn regarded me with raised eyebrows.

"I'm fine." I twisted in my chair and looked out the window behind me. "I just ..."

"Nell, let me assure you, you're not trading one prison for another. We thought we'd lay out some plans, and then you're free to look around, get to know the place. Zoe would like to do some training with you outside, if you think you might be up to it today."

"Okay." I took a deep breath. "So, plans. What are they? How do you intend to use me to save Rafe?"

Zoe leaned forward. "I want you to understand, we're not using you. We hope that using your abilities can help us rescue him. But we intend for you to be part of the planning process."

I nodded. "All right then. What have you come up with so far?"

The two women exchanged glances before Cathryn spoke. "The first thing we'd like you to try is projecting to the camp where they're holding Rafe, so that we can get a general lay of the land, see where he's being held. Once we know that, whomever we send in to make the save will have a better idea of what he's up against. We can be more prepared."

"I want to be the one to go in." I said it with finality, in the old Nell Massler voice that brooked no dissent. "You brought me out of my coma and—activated me, for lack of a better word—for this mission. I don't want to just do recon. I need to be the one to rescue Rafe. I know I *can* do it."

Zoe smiled. "I fully expected you to say that."

"She did." Cathryn rolled her eyes. "She's going to do her I-told-you-so dance the minute we're alone. Thanks for that."

"But I'm going to do it." I didn't know when or where I'd made this decision, but it felt right and solid, the first thing to feel that way in so long. My mother had chosen madness and a man over me, and my father had walked away and then thrown me away. Marica had used me until the real thing—in the form of Tasmyn—came along, and then she dropped me, too.

But Cathryn, and then Zoe, by association, had chosen me. Wanted me, and even if it were only for my abilities, I didn't care. I was going to do whatever I could to prove that they weren't wrong. I could do this.

"We'll discuss it." Cathryn pulled out a tablet and swiped it on. "I'd like to go over what we know first, and then we'll talk about our first move."

She angled the screen so that I could see a map, but it was just a network of lines and squares. I frowned, trying to follow her words.

"This is where the camp is. What we know is that Rafe

and Jocelyn were able to infiltrate the community. What we don't know is how much they discovered before ... before everything went bad. We hope that once Rafe is safe and healthy, he can shed some light on the activities and plans of this group."

"Do we have a name for these people?" I pointed at the map. "Or do you just keep calling them the bad guys?"

Zoe huffed out a laugh but sobered quickly, shaking her head. "We know they're somehow connected with Ben Ryan, Congressman Remington's campaign manager who was trying to frame your father. It seems he was at the very least luring people into the commune. They control two munitions factories that we know of: one outside Savannah, and the other near New Orleans. What they plan to do with the weapons is less than clear. We're not sure if they're selling them on the black market or distributing them internationally ... or just hoarding them."

"Not knowing is frustrating. What we suspect is frankly terrifying." Cathryn flipped her fingers over the screen of the tablet again, and this time a chart appeared. There were boxes, each containing a name or a set of words, and connected to each other by lines.

"This is the network as far as we've figured it out, from the information we took out of Ben's computer, and from the legwork our other agents have done. We have hints and hunches, but we don't know all the players or what their ultimate goal is. The fact that it's so involved and complicated makes us believe that this has been in the works for a long time."

I skimmed the screen. "My father's name is on this. Do you think he's part of it?"

Cathryn shook her head. "I really don't. He's only there because of his connection to Remington, and Remington's connection to Ryan." She touched a switch and turned off the tablet. "I just wanted you to see the scope of what we're up against. Our number one short-term goal, of course, is Rafe's safety. We want him out of the camp. But at the same time, we need to protect this organization. We have agents in dangerous situations all over the world who could be compromised if this group decides to target Carruthers. These people aren't amateurs, Nell. This Mallory Jones—she can kill just by thinking about it. She's not getting her hands dirty. She's powerful, and she works for the bad guys."

"I get it. Caution. And plausible deniability. Can we talk specifics?"

Cathryn sucked in a breath through her nose. "Are you sure about this, Nell? Do you want to take some time and reconsider?"

"No, I want to make a plan, and I want to move on this. You said your —what did you call her? Precog? She thinks they're planning to kill Rafe. I need to be up there saving him, like yesterday."

Zoe nodded. "I agree. The first thing we need to do is that reconnaissance. Are you feeling up to a little astral projection, Nell?"

I swallowed. "You said there might be a way to do it without blood."

"Absolutely. I researched what you had been looking at in King, and I found the crystals. They might help. But I have a few other ideas, too."

"Great. Let's do it."

"Nell, you just got out of the hospital. Maybe we should

give you a little time."

"Does Rafe have a little time?"

Cathryn's eyes met Zoe's over my head, and I saw the answer.

"That's what I thought. Let's do it now."

Zoe thought it was important that we work where we wouldn't be disturbed, so I followed her back downstairs and into a large room lined with bookshelves. I sank down into the armchair she indicated.

"I have the crystals." She reached under the table and pulled out a box. "I don't know how much help they'll be, but it won't hurt to have them here." She arranged the boxy lime-green rocks on one side of the mahogany table and then added a few glossy jet-black orbs between them.

"Rhodizite and black tourmaline? Interesting."

"From what I've read, they're the most effective."

The door opened and Cathryn joined us, shutting it behind her with a soft click.

"Are we ready, ladies?"

"Just about." Zoe looked at the crystal arrangement with narrowed eyes and then moved one of the rhodizites half an inch to the left. "Pull up that chair, please, Cathryn. We need to be close enough to reach Nell."

Cathryn dragged over the mate to my seat. "Are you comfortable, Nell? Is there anything else you need to do before we get started?"

I raised one eyebrow. "I used the bathroom and washed my hands if that's what you mean."

"No, I meant are you safe in the chair? Do we need to strap you in or anything? Will you fall over once you're gone?"

Zoe sighed. "She'll be fine, Cathryn. Worst case, she may slump a little, but we'll make sure she doesn't fall."

"I don't know what happens after I'm gone. Every time before, I was bleeding. I woke up in the bed, usually with some nurse screaming at me about how I did it. Or I'd be sedated and not wake up for a day or two."

"Ah." Zoe nodded. "Of course. Well, this time I can guarantee we won't have you in a bed or drugged. We'll be right here with you the whole time."

"All right." I inhaled and closed my eyes. "So I'm going to focus on the location of the camp as you showed it to me, and on Rafe. But remember I've never done it this way. I don't know Rafe. And each time I visited Tasmyn, it was at a place we'd been together. The last time, I was so anxious and had so much adrenalin, I think that and the extra blood gave me the push."

"This time, you have the crystals. And you have us." She smiled at me. "Focus."

My mind moved to the image I had of the camp. I fastened on it, willed myself there. I reached out a hand to cover the crystals nearest to me, and that contact loosened me from my moorings. I could feel myself beginning to rise, to float ... but I wasn't going anywhere.

"Relax, Nell. Know we are here with you." I felt Zoe's hand on my arm, and Cathryn's on my shoulder, and then the most intense flare of power filled me, tingling through every fiber of my body. I could sense both Cathryn and Zoe connected to me, and I knew they were giving me the extra boost I needed to make this happen.

I was sucked into some kind of funnel. My mind was squeezed and pushed, and I had the sensation of being spun, like when I'd gone on the tilt-o-whirl at the carnival as a little girl. And then everything stopped with such force that I was sure my head was about to hit the ground.

I opened my eyes. Sunlight assaulted me, and I moved to step into the shade of the trees a few feet away. I stood on the side of a road, with nothing but tall pines in every direction.

The world shimmered around me when I turned my head or moved, just as it had when I used to visit Tasmyn. It was almost like being underwater, with the colors muted and sound traveling at an odd speed. I took a moment to settle into my new surroundings and then slipped into the forest, in what I hoped was the direction of the camp.

I ran into a small tent first, and if I had been solid, I might have tripped. As it was, my foot passed through the peg that anchored it to the forest floor. It didn't look as though anyone had been in it for a long time. Leaves had collected at the base, and a thin sheen of dirt and pollen coated the door flaps. Out of habit, I went to push aside the flaps before I remembered I could simply lean in.

Two sleeping bags lay on the ground, along side a black duffel bag. When I looked closer, I saw a tag on the handle, with a name in strong slanted handwriting: Jocelyn Pennell. My heart thumped; this must have been her tent.

But ... two sleeping bags. And in the corner of the tent, someone had tossed a black shaving kit bag. It could have been Jocelyn's, but I knew it wasn't. It was Rafe's.

I began making my way along the path again, thinking. It made sense that Rafe and Jocelyn would pose as a couple for this mission, so I didn't know why I was surprised. Cathryn and Zoe hadn't given me all the details of their assignment, other than they were supposed to get information on the movement of the weapons and the role of the so-called commune.

"Goddammit, Ian. We don't have time to mess around. Time's short. Mallory's going to be back tomorrow, and we need to be ready to move."

I nearly ducked behind a tree before I remembered that the two men I heard couldn't see me. At least, I didn't think they could. I stepped closer, grateful that my non-corporeal form didn't crunch leaves or snap twigs.

"I know that. But we need to get him out of here before she comes. He's from a rich family, and they're going to come looking for him sooner or later. If they find his body here, and link us with that ..." Ian ran a hand through his gray hair and darted his eyes back and forth around the small clearing where they stood.

The first man laughed. "Never gonna happen, and even if it does, won't matter. By the time they find him, the world will be burning. Last thing anyone will worry about is some stupid rich kid who got lost in the woods and died."

"Easy for you to say. You're leaving with them. I've got to hang back and organize the drones, and I don't feel like dealing with cops or the government. It's easy. All we got to do is just toss him off on the side of the road somewhere or leave him on a sidewalk in Savannah. He's half-dead anyway. More than likely no one will listen to him, or he could even be gone before he can talk."

I could see them better now. The guy who wasn't Ian was shorter, but he was still an imposing figure. He was stocky, with a thick neck and muscled shoulders.

"Too risky. It's already planned for tomorrow. Mallory gets here, she zaps him, and then we're on our way." He clapped Ian on the back. "And don't worry, you won't be far behind. We're going to need you and your drones in the trenches. This is gonna happen, man. It's real. Can't you feel it?"

Ian snorted. "All I feel is like I'm being set up as the fall guy. And what am I going to tell Cara when she finds out about Brooks? She threw a shit fit when she found out what Mallory did to the girl. She treated them like crap when they got here, but in the end, they're old friends of hers. At least Brooks is. She's the only reason Nathan hasn't shot him in that hole. She threatened to go to Ben—"

"Ben's not in the picture. You know that. Cara can bitch and say whatever she wants about him coming back, but Nathan told me it isn't going to happen. He's gone. So you don't need to be afraid of Cara." The way he glanced around as he spoke told me he didn't quite buy his own words.

Something clicked in my mind as his words filtered in. *Cara.* There had been a girl in King by that name, someone I had known even before Tasmyn had moved to town. She'd been a newcomer, too. I didn't remember too much about the girl, but I wondered if it could possibly be the same person. Ian said they had been old friends.

The two men turned in the opposite direction from me and tramped through the foliage. I kept behind, just to be on the safe side, and followed the sounds of people talking. I needed to find out where Rafe was being held and how closely he was guarded. I had to figure out the easiest way to get him out of here ... before tomorrow.

The woods opened to a large clearing that was bordered by a massive log cabin. A fire pit was in the center of the space, but in the heat of the summer day, it was cold and empty. A few people wandered around, and I could hear others talking from inside the cabin. But no sign of a hole or of Rafe.

The screen door of the cabin opened and banged shut behind a familiar girl who was about my age. I sucked in a gasp.

"Shit, it really is her." I spoke out loud without thinking about it.

Cara looked around the clearing. She was carrying a brown paper bag, and as she walked quickly toward a path leading around the house, she clutched it to her chest.

Following her seemed like a good bet. According to Ian and his nameless buddy, Cara was against killing Rafe. It stood to reason that she might be trying to help him, even if she didn't want any of her new wacky anarchist friends to know it.

I followed behind her, trying to ignore the slightly queasy feeling the passing trees gave me. They bled together like running water-colors and made me a little off-balanced.

Cara kept on going, even when we came to a smaller cabin. She made her way around it, past a padlocked shed and back into the woods. I made mental notes of the landmarks so I could find my way there tomorrow.

Tomorrow. Good Christ, this was going to happen sooner than I thought. I wasn't nearly ready. I was only just out of the hospital. I gritted my teeth and plunged on after Cara's retreating back.

She stopped at a place where the trees were sparser, and when she took a few steps off the path, I could see mounds of dirt at the end of a worn, narrow trail. Cara knelt down and began to open the bag. I craned my neck and saw that she was leaning over the edge of hole in the ground.

"Rafe, it's me. I brought you food. I'm sorry it took so long. Can you hear me?" She paused, waiting. I didn't hear anything but the birds chirping around us.

"I'm sorry. I'm sorry they did this. I mean, you shouldn't have been here, and Mallory says you came here to stop the plan. I don't know what's going on with you, and I don't know why you're here, but I don't want you to die. I didn't want Joss to die, either."

Cara reached into the bag and withdrew a roll and something else in a small paper towel-wrapped package. She dropped them both into the hole and watched. I wondered if Rafe were awake, and if he even acknowledged her presence. After a moment, she lowered a bottle of water down, and I heard a thud as it hit the bottom.

"That's all I can do. We're getting ready to leave the camp. But a few people are staying behind, and I've talked to Ian. He's going to take care of you after Nathan and I leave. I'll try to send help. But Rafe, if you can hear this, you've got to leave us alone and stay out of our way. This plan is bigger than you could imagine, and nothing can stop us now. It's all going to be good, especially for people like you. People with powers. Trust me."

Cara rose to her feet and brushed off the seat of her shorts. She looked back over her shoulder, and for a chilling moment, I was certain that she saw me. But she didn't react; she only crumpled the paper back in her hand and walked away, her head down.

I needed to get back to Carruthers. I had to tell Zoe and Cathryn what I'd learned and somehow get up here before Rafe's time ran out. But I knew I had to check one more thing before I left.

I floated along the path Cara had just vacated and stood as near the edge of the hole as I dared. The trees blocked most of the light, but I could just make out a form below. He lay on his side, curled in the fetal position. I stared, willing him to move, to give me some positive proof of life. Just when I was about to give up, his leg straightened against the side of his prison.

A flood of relief washed over me. I wanted to call down to him, to reassure him that help was on its way, but on the other hand, I wasn't sure he could hear my voice ... and if I could be heard, the last thing I needed was to attract attention.

I rose, preparing to let go of this place and return to Harper Creek. But as I did, my eye caught another mound of dirt. It was long and narrow, recently overturned, only a few feet from the edge of the hole where Rafe lay. Revulsion filled me as I realized what it had to be.

It was Jocelyn's grave.

I swallowed down fury. These people ... they weren't any better than animals, leaving Rafe out here in the ground, for God's sake, lying in his own filth, exposed to the weather as they tossed food down to him. But to dig that hole alongside the grave of his murdered friend was beyond cruel. It was horrible.

Did he know, I wondered? Or was he so far gone that he didn't even realize what was happening anymore?

I backed up into the trees once more and closed my eyes, breathing deeply. Link by tenuous link, I let go of this location. As I was sucked back into the swirling vacuum, I sent Rafe a message, knowing full well he couldn't hear me, yet somehow needing to say it.

Don't give up. I'm coming to save you.

CHAPTER
6

CONSCIOUSNESS SLAMMED BACK INTO my body with a jolt, and my head rocked into the top of the chair.

"Nell?" Zoe leaned over me, peering into my face. "Are you all right?"

I breathed in and out, letting the feeling come back into my fingers and toes. "I'm okay." I licked my lips and let my heart slow to a reasonable rate. "I am. I'm okay."

"Did you make it there?" Cathryn's voice was anxious.

"Yeah." I flexed my hands. "I did. I was in the camp, and I saw Rafe. He's alive."

Both women sat back in their chairs, a measure of relief evident on their faces. I hated to take that away from them, but they had to understand just how little time we had.

"But he won't be for long. They plan to kill him tomorrow." I ran down a brief synopsis of what I'd heard in Georgia.

Cathryn closed her eyes. "Tomorrow. There's no way ... unless we contact the authorities and convince them to go into the camp, and even then, Rafe would be dead as soon as those people realized they were compromised."

Zoe looked more somber than I'd ever seen her. "Nell, Cara Pryce was there? I know her from both Rafe and Tasmyn's stories. How odd that she's involved in this mess."

"She's the only thing keeping Rafe alive, according to the men I overheard." I straightened in the chair. "But that ends tomorrow. That's why I have to go in. How fast can you get me up to Georgia?"

"Nell, there's no way ..." Cathryn began to speak at the same time Zoe did.

"What do you need to save him?"

Cathryn glared at the other woman. "Are you crazy? We can't send her in there, one day out of the hospital, a week or so out of a coma. It's like handing her a death sentence. I'm not losing another one, Zoe. I can't."

"If we don't let her try, Rafe is dead. Are you willing to let that happen? I'm not. Cathryn, Nell can do this. She's stronger than you realize. And with the proper motivation, which I think she has now, I know she can save him."

"I need to practice." I'd been thinking about it since hearing the men on the commune. "I have a plan, but I have to be sure I can pull it off. Is there some place here I can work, where no one will see me? And where I can do some damage?"

"What kind of damage?" Cathryn quirked an eyebrow.

"Ripping up trees from their roots."

Cathryn made me stay inside the house with them while she and Zoe sketched out a plan for my trip to Georgia. I sat on the edge of my seat, my knees bouncing up and down from nerves, as I listened to the two of them.

"We need to play this as close to the vest as possible. The fewer people who know about the rescue, the better."

"Do you think you have another mole?" I glanced at her.

"No, I don't. We've beefed up security since Emma. But this organization has powers that we might not expect. If they don't have qualms about murder, I doubt they'll mind using our own people against us. We don't want to give them opportunity to do that."

"So only five of us will know you're going in tomorrow, Nell. The three of us, Harley and my father." Cathryn pinched the bridge of her nose and closed her eyes. "I'll handle them while you and Zoe work outside."

"She'll need a vehicle to get up there, Cathryn." Zoe was making notes on a yellow legal tablet. "Something that's not traceable to Carruthers."

"We'll arrange that. Nell, you have to understand that once you're up there, you cannot have any communication with us. We can't have the Institute connected to you. If—when—you and Rafe get out of there, you can't come back here right away. Not until we know more about the plans these lunatics have." Cathryn's jaw tightened. "God, we need to know more. It's not just a weapons ring. They're trying to destroy the world."

"We're going to stop them." Zoe squeezed her hand. "But first things first. Nell, is there some place you could go after you leave the camp? Don't tell me where," she added. "Just say yes or no."

"I don't know. You mean like a safe house?"

"It has to be somewhat hidden and yes, safe. Carruthers

has a few, but we can't risk that."

I searched my memory. I couldn't take Rafe back to King, a place that was linked to both of us. And where else had I been during the first eighteen years of my life?

"Well, think about it. Meanwhile, we'll go outside and practice while Cathryn works her own magic."

We left Cathryn muttering to herself about people expecting her to be a freaking miracle worker.

"Don't mind her." Zoe held the door for me, and I walked into the sunshine, blinking.

"She doesn't think I can do it."

"No, she's worried. Cathryn likes her life in order. What you're proposing to do is so far outside her control, it makes her nervous. She knows, as I do, that if things go very wrong, we can't do anything to help you. And even if you get out alive, both of you, we may not know for a long time."

"This organization ... Ben's group. It's that big? That powerful?"

"I'm afraid it is." Zoe led me to a garage just beyond the parking lot. "Now hold that thought. I don't want to say anything in front of Ken. He handles all our cars, and of course we trust him, but again ... let's not put anyone at risk unnecessarily."

"We need a car?" I thought we were staying on the Carruthers property.

"Shhh." Zoe laid a finger on her lips and called out. "Ken! Do you have a cart Nell and I can use?"

A man's head appeared around a doorway. "Zoe! For you, my love, anything. Even the Maserati."

"Ah, Ken, you'll break my heart. Just a cart today. Nell and I are going to work at the far edge of the property."

"Have fun." He stepped out and scanned the peg board, and then snagged a set of keys from the hook. "Right outside, all charged up. Be careful."

I understood his warning as Zoe drove over the bumpy paths. The golf cart could only go twenty miles an hour, but she kept her foot to the floor the whole way.

"God, Zoe! You're going to wreck us." I clung to the bar. "You almost dumped me out back there on that curve."

"We don't have time to go slow today." She shot me a wicked smile. "Not that I would anyway. I like to go fast. Joss used to say—" She stopped speaking abruptly, and her lips tightened as tears filled her eyes. She swallowed hard before going on. "She used to say I had a need for speed. She did, too. We loved to drive together."

She slowed and brought the cart to a stop at the edge of a field. Neither of us moved for a minute, and then I reached over and laid my hand on Zoe's where her fingers clenched the steering wheel.

"I'm sorry, Zoe."

"I know." She managed a smile, sniffing. "I think part of me still had hope, no matter what Fee had said. Maybe she was wrong. But after what you heard and saw ... I know she was right. Joss is really and truly gone."

"Zoe, I wanted to ask you about Joss and Rafe. Were they posing as a couple to go undercover? Was that part of their mission?"

She nodded. "Yes. But it was more than that. They did have a relationship. Joss recruited Rafe, and at first I think they were just having fun. But before they left for Georgia, I saw something else between them. More than just friends, more than just fun. I wanted to talk to you about that, because if you're able to rescue Rafe, you'll have to deal with not only his physical injuries, but also with his grief over her loss, as well. It's not going to be easy."

I rolled my eyes. "Zoe, no offense, but if I get us both out of there, Rafe's mental health is going to be the least of my worries."

"You might think so now, but if you have to stay hidden with him for any length of time, it's going to be an issue. We haven't gone into great detail with you about Rafe's story. You knew he had a relationship with Tasmyn, yes?"

"Yeah. I had a front row seat to that one. Via Tasmyn's mind, I mean."

"That's right. Well, Rafe didn't do so well after she broke his heart. They both had healing to do, it's true, but Tasmyn had Michael, and Rafe was alone. He went on wild spree last summer. We followed him around this country, just waiting for him to finish sowing his oats so we could recruit him. And what he had with Tas was not nearly as strong as what he felt for Jocelyn."

"What do you want me to do about it?" I needed to focus on one thing at a time, and right now, that one thing was saving Rafe. Making sure he didn't end up dead. His broken heart was way beyond the scope of my abilities.

"I want you to be aware. Rafe may not want to be saved. He may not see any reason to go on. From what Fee told us, it seems Joss was killed right in front of him. That's going to be an enormous trauma for him to get over."

"So are you going to give me shrink lessons? Do you really think that's high on the priority list right now, Zoe?"

"Maybe not. But you should know that Rafe has grandparents in King. He is very close to them. They are his family, more so than his mother at this point. You may need to remind him of that. Giving him a reason to keep breathing could be a challenge."

I nodded. "Okay, sure. I got it." I climbed out of the golf cart. "Now can we rip up some trees?"

Letting go, giving my power free rein, felt good. I had been holding back in the hospital, worried about my lack of control and of scaring off Zoe and Cathryn. But now, with frustration and anger rolling through my system, everything came easily.

"Why trees?" Zoe watched as I made a new path in the dense forest.

"The camp is in the middle of the woods. I need to go in with the biggest element of surprise I can manage, and starting off by knocking down the whole damn thing is a good start."

"Excellent point. And then what?"

"And then ..." I focused on the small pile of branches fifteen feet away from us, and they burst into flames. "That's distraction."

"I'll say." Zoe eyed the fire. "Want to put that out before we have the forest service out here?"

"Sure." I reached below the dirt, deep under the surface, and pulled up a column of water that shot out onto the branches. They settled to a smolder.

"Anything else?"

"I have one more trick up my sleeve. Are you ready?"

Zoe had the good sense to look a little frightened. "For

what?"

"Grab hold of that rock and watch the line of trees over there." I jerked my chin in the direction of the green tops on the rise further away from us. A moment later, the ground shook beneath us as the trees vanished from our sight.

"What did you do?" Zoe was a little pale as she stared at the hill.

"Split the earth. Like an earthquake, but more localized. It's not really effective, but it's damned scary, isn't it?"

"Oh, yes." Zoe stood up again, not quite steady yet. "Nell, I wish Cathryn had seen you out here. I think she would feel much more assured about your chances."

"I feel better myself." I threw back my head and breathed deep. I felt exhilarated and alive for the first time in so long. The wind blew over me, and I reached out to it, encouraged it to grow a little stronger. My hair swirled over my face as I threw out my arms.

When I opened my eyes and looked at Zoe, she was smiling at me, an odd expression on her face.

"I can feel the power surrounding you. I've been working with extraordinary people for a long time. I don't think I've ever known anyone quite like you."

I smirked. "That's not the first time I've heard that."

"I mean it. You're incredibly talented." She gazed out to where the sun was beginning to sink lower in the sky. "Nell, as much as you're taking a chance with Carruthers, with trusting us, remember that we're doing the same with you. I trust you, and so does Cathryn. But there will be temptation along the way. Someone might offer you the chance to use your powers more fully, tell you that we're holding you back or keeping you from being who you truly are. I want you to remember what you know right now. This is your second chance. Don't waste it."

I nodded, sober now. "I know. And I promise, Zoe, I'm not going to let you down. I'm going to rescue Rafe and keep Carruthers safe. I won't make you and Cathryn regret this."

CHAPTER 7

I LEFT HARPER CREEK JUST after midnight. Cathryn had worked miracles and presented me with a valid driver's license, since mine had lapsed while I was hospitalized and comatose. I was both eager and apprehensive about getting behind the wheel again.

"I should take you for a test drive before you leave." Cathryn's face had been in perpetual worry-mode since we'd decided I was going to Georgia. "Just around here, on the property."

"Oh, cool! I can drive your car?" I bit back a smile when her face went from concern to absolute terror. "I'm joking, Cathryn. I'll be fine. I was a good driver before ... before I was crazy."

"Besides, she needs sleep more than driving practice." Zoe looked at her watch. "I'd like you to get in a solid six hours before you leave."

Cathryn bit her lip. "There's so much I still need to brief you on. Zoe, did you talk to her about Rafe's relationship with ...?"

Zoe nodded. "We went over Rafe's possible mental and emotional states and how best to deal with them. She has Rafe's file to look over tonight in the ..." She glanced at her watch again. "... twenty minutes before she needs to be asleep."

"Are you sure I need to sleep? Maybe I should just get started up there now. If I could get into the camp before sunrise, it might give me another advantage. Get them while they're all still in bed. Anyway, I just woke up from a really long coma-nap. Haven't I slept enough?"

Cathryn shook her head. "Zoe's right. You need to have a little rest under your belt before you make that drive. Falling asleep at the wheel and ending up dead in a ditch isn't going to help anyone."

I tilted my head and laid a hand over my heart. "Cathryn, any more sweet talk and I'm going to start thinking about taking our relationship to the next level."

"This is not a joke, Nell. It's life or death for both you and Rafe. Do you think these people are playing a game? Do you think if they catch you, they're going to pat you on the head and send you home? No. You'll be dead. In a hole next to Jocelyn and Rafe."

The silence that smothered the room was thick. Zoe cleared her throat and patted my back.

"We're all stressed right now, and Cathryn and I are quite anxious. Even if we'd had weeks to prepare you for this mission, we wouldn't feel that you were ready. We're tossing you to the wolves. At this point, all we can do is send you up there in the best condition possible. That means sleep and food. There's a bed upstairs, turned down and waiting for you. And Henry's putting together a meal for you take on the road."

Zoe took me upstairs and handed me Rafe's file, promising to return shortly to take it back so that I would sleep. The bedroom I'd been assigned was in a different wing of the manor than were the library and other public rooms. It was all dark wood and heavy drapes, ripe with age and yet comfortable. I climbed into the four-poster and leaned against a pile of pillows before I opened Rafe's file.

In the interest of time, Zoe had organized it so that the most vital information was in the front. I skimmed the papers, trying to memorize what I needed to know. Rafe had had an eventful year. I read the accounts of his summer travels with raised eyebrows—the boy had gotten *around*—and then tackled the report Joss had written of their time together in New Orleans.

Those pages gave me almost as much insight into the Carruthers agent as it did into Rafe. Her humor and personality shone through the words, and I felt an odd regret that I would never meet her.

By the time Zoe came back, hand outstretched for the papers, some of the nerves she and Cathryn were feeling had jumped onto me. My shoulders tensed up to my ears, and the thought of sleep was laughable.

"Nell, lie down." Zoe sat on the edge of the mattress. "You need sleep. Now. Close your eyes."

"But Zoe—"

"Shhh." She moved her hand to my head, and a wave of drowsiness almost drowned me. I blinked and then my eyes didn't open again until Cathryn shook my shoulder just as a clock somewhere in the house was striking midnight.

"I brought you some clothes to wear tonight, and I

packed a bag for you, too. It's in the trunk of the car. Henry's put together a basket of food, and we left it on the front seat for easy access."

"Thanks." I stretched and yawned, but I actually felt good. Must have been some Zoe mojo. I made a mental note to call her next time I had insomnia. If I lived for there to be a next time.

"Here." Cathryn thrust a small black phone into my hand. "This is a burner. It was purchased with cash a hundred miles south of here, and there is one number loaded into it. Our tech people swear it can't be traced to us."

"Okay." I took the phone. "Why?"

"If—no, when. When you and Rafe get away from that camp, I want you to text the word 'yes' to that number. And then destroy the phone. Stomp it, run over it with a car, whatever you have to do. Make sure you don't do it any place near where you end up hiding out. Got it?"

"Yes. Speaking of which, I think I know where I'll take him. I had a dream last night—I mean, while I was sleeping just now. And I remembered—"

"No." Cathryn held out one hand. "Don't tell me. None of us can know."

"How will you get in touch with us when it's safe for us to come back then?"

"You'll buy a disposable telephone periodically and use the number in the burner I gave you—memorize it. Text us a question mark. Wait five minutes. If something has changed, we'll text you back. If you don't hear from us in that five minutes, get rid of the phone. Is that clear?"

I nodded. "Perfectly."

"Good. Don't forget to keep your blocks up at all times.

Remember, these are not ordinary people. Oh, and there's also cash in the bag for you. Can you think of anything I've missed?"

"I can't imagine there could be. Cathryn, you really are amazing. I can't believe you pulled all of this together so fast. And I want you to know something." I fiddled with a button the shirt she'd laid out for me. "If I don't make it back from this mission, I'm okay. The fact that you stood up for me, that you went out of your way to bring me into Carruthers, is probably the nicest thing anyone has ever done for me. If I can pull this off and bring Rafe home, it'll only be because you believed I could. Or at least you made me think you did."

Cathryn's back stiffened and her jaw clenched. "Nell Massler, by God, if you go up there and get yourself killed after I went to bat for you with my father not once but twice ... I swear, I will never forgive you."

I knew she was trying to lighten the moment, but I couldn't manage a smile. I nodded once.

"Understood."

"Good. Now get dressed and meet me downstairs."

Zoe and Cathryn stood silent when I found them in the dim light of the kitchen. Before I could stop her, Zoe folded me into her arms, hugging me close. My breath caught; I didn't think anyone had held me like this since my mother. I forced my body to relax in her embrace, and she touched my cheek as she backed away.

"Go in peace, my dear. I have every confidence in you. I'll see you—and Rafe—shortly."

Cathryn dangled the car keys. "I think you're set. I'll look forward to your text tomorrow. Drive safely, please."

There was no hug from her, but she did hold my hand an extra moment as she pressed the keys into my palm. I stepped into the black velvet of the night and glanced back for just a moment at the two women watching me. Their faces were inscrutable, yet flowing from them, I felt love and belief like I hadn't known for decades.

I climbed into the dark sedan and turned the key. Within moments, I was out on the road, heading north.

I had projected myself to the remote camp in Georgia in a matter of nanoseconds, so the fact that it took me four hours to get there via car was monotonous. The roads were relatively empty except for the occasional passing trucks. I stuck to the speed limit; even if I thought I could get away with going faster, it wasn't worth the risk of getting pulled over and possibly leaving a record of my trip.

The sky was still pitch black when I reached the last lonely road on my GPS directions. It ran between two swamps that were dotted with clumps of scrub pines, and there was not another landmark as far as I could see. I pulled to the shoulder and turned off my lights. I wasn't certain how far I had to walk to reach the commune, and the knots in my stomach reminded me that I didn't know how much time I had, either. Or more accurately, how much time Rafe had.

I climbed out of the car, locking the door behind me. The remains of the meal Henry had made me were in the wicker basket on the front seat, and I knew in the Georgia heat, it wasn't going to smell pretty once I got back to the car—if I got back to the car. I decided that if I did make it out alive, the smell of last night's dinner would be the least of my worries.

It was the 'if' that got me. Driving right into the camp would be tantamount to suicide, I knew that. But Rafe was in bad shape. I wasn't sure how I was going to get him from that hole in the ground back to the car, which made me think that I had to plan for the possibility that I wasn't going to leave the same way I'd arrived. I knew they had to have vehicles on the property somewhere, and if I could get one of those ... it might be my only real chance for escape.

I opened the trunk and unzipped the duffle Cathryn had packed for me. There was no way I could lug this thing along with me, and if I had to carry Rafe—I grimaced—I wouldn't be able to manage the bag, too. I thrust my hand inside and found the cash Cathryn had tucked among the clothes. Good thing the outfit Cathryn had given me had extra pockets; I distributed the bills among all of them and zipped the burner phone, along with my new driver's license, into an interior one.

And then there was nothing else to do. There was a faint glow just barely visible in the eastern sky that told me the sun would be rising in an hour or so. I had no idea what time Mallory Jones was going to get to the camp, but leaving before her arrival really wouldn't upset me at all. Being miles up the road with Rafe safely in tow would make me a happy girl.

Each of my footsteps crunching in the dried grass was deafening to me. After the freedom of floating around soundlessly the day before, I felt clumsy and awkward picking my way between the trees.

Every few minutes, I stopped and listened, craning both

my ears and my inner antennae to see if I could pick up sounds of life or the trace of energy that accompanied people with extraordinary abilities. I walked for at least twenty minutes before I felt something, just the faintest trace of spark coming from somewhere to my right. I cocked my head, listening. A few seconds later, I made out the sound of voices. I couldn't discern what they were saying, but it was a conversation.

I stepped more carefully, avoiding the leaves and pausing between each movement. Every fiber of my body was alert; the merest brush of wind spiked my adrenalin, and my senses were on high alert. When I heard voices again, this time much closer to me, I froze and stood behind a tree.

"... they just went to get him. Nathan said Mallory is close, and she should be here before daylight. I'd like to see how they haul his body out of that hole. He sure as hell isn't going to cooperate."

The second voice belonged to a woman. "Why don't they just leave him down there and do it? Toss in the dirt on top."

"Too close to Cara and Nathan's cabin. Nathan's going to try to get Cara out the back way, distract her, so they can get him to the clearing. And Ian said Mallory wants people to see it, too. Like an example, I guess."

I squinted into the distance. So they were going to get Rafe out of the ground. That was a relief. I had wondered how I was going to make that happen. And the clearing ... I remembered the huge log cabin I'd seen the day before, with the fire pit and seating area in front. If I had to choose a spot in the camp for a public execution, that would be it.

The two people moved on, and I waited until I couldn't

hear them anymore before I followed. Through the trees, I spotted a narrow dirt road that ended in an open lot. A few skeletons of ancient cars bordered the parking area, but I spotted two others that had potential. One was an old car that reminded me a little of Michael Sawyer's vintage Mustang, but I wasn't sure what make it was. To me, one car looked pretty much like another.

I skirted the lot and stuck to the woods alongside the path. The farther I walked, the more intense the sensations of other powers became. I concentrated on maintaining my blocks. If they picked me up before I could get Rafe, we were both screwed.

The clearing was just in front of me. My eyes had adjusted to the half-light, and I could see the large cabin through the trees. As I watched, two men stumbled out of the woods opposite me, dragging a something between them. I leaned a little further in, peering at the figures as they dropped a body on the ground.

Rafe. I drew in a deep breath. It was now or never. If what I'd heard a few minutes earlier was accurate, Mallory Jones could be here already.

"Hey. What are you doing?"

Panic sliced through me as I turned. A man with brown hair curling beneath the edge of his red baseball cap was looking at me with surprise and curiosity. He was wearing worn shorts and a faded t-shirt, but he didn't look threatening, and he wasn't coming toward me. I wasn't getting any sense of super powers, either.

Part of me was tempted to just come up with some explanation, some reason for why I was in this camp in the middle of fucking nowhere. Something this guy, who didn't strike me as the sharpest tool in the shed, might buy without issue. But before I could open my mouth to put plan-charm-the-good-ol'-boy into action, I heard another voice behind him.

"Billy, who the hell you talking to? Get over here and give me a hand." A taller man with gray hair stepped off the path. His eyes met mine over Billy's head, and I realized two things: one, this was Ian, one of the men I'd overheard talking the day before; and two, he was much more dangerous than Billy was. My come-in-quiet option disintegrated in front of my face.

He opened his mouth to yell—I could see it in his eyes, he was raising the alarm—and I didn't think. I reacted. A burst of energy exploded from me, and the larger man flew across path behind him, hitting a tree.

I caught my breath and turned to run toward the clearing. Billy yelled, and I didn't hesitate to push him down as well. Ian was beginning to struggle to his feet, and I felt him gathering strength. I dipped into the well of anger and uprooted a tree, tossing it over the two men. I felt a little twinge of regret for Billy, but on the other hand, collateral damage was inevitable in this situation.

And now that it had begun, the volcano of power erupted within me. The thought of these people, who had killed an innocent girl and were holding Rafe prisoner, intending to murder him, too, enraged me. I hadn't realized I was capable of feeling such a level of fury on behalf of other people. It felt right, and good, that everything I'd been holding back and trying to control was letting loose.

Trees flew, landing with resounding crashes on top of tents. The few cabins in the rest of the forest fell victim to heavy trunks and branches. I heard screams echo beyond me, and they only served to incite more anger. I wanted them to burn now, and as I thought it, fire erupted ten feet away from me, catching the pine needles and the wildly stacked trees. Already dry from the summer heat, they flamed, catching with a loud *whoop* that shook me.

"What's going on? What's happening?" Feet were running both toward me and away from me as chaos woke the camp.

A black-haired man spied me as I stood on the edge of the path, just inside the tree line. He charged me like a bull who had seen red, but deflecting him didn't even distract me. I extended the block I was holding tight around my mind to encompass my entire body, and he bounced away from as though he'd hit concrete.

Between the sun rising and the trees I'd removed, it was easier to see into the clearing now. The men who had tossed Rafe to the ground still stood over him, even as screams of "Fire!" sounded all around. I decided it was time to shake things up a little more.

The earth shook, and this time, cracks split the clearing, separating it from the cabin. I narrowed my eyes at the wooden building and smiled a little as it rumbled and then exploded. There was a gas generator there, and it didn't play well with the fire I'd just ignited under the porch.

The men guarding Rafe fell as the world tilted again. I waited until they'd scrambled to their feet and run away wildly, limbs flying, before I made one more mental sweep of the camp.

The screaming had stopped when the earth tremors began, but I sensed people were still nearby. I sent one more sweep of fire and quakes before the world fell silent.

Adrenalin surged through my veins, and I kicked a branch out of my way as I stalked into the clearing. Rafe lay face down in the dirt, his arms spread out. For a dizzy moment, I wasn't sure he was still alive. And then I saw the slightest rise of his back as he breathed.

As I approached him, the stench of filth almost made me gag. He didn't move at all, and I wasn't sure if he were even conscious. And of course, he didn't know me. We'd never met in King, since I was already in the loony bin when he moved to town. He might have thought I was just another person from the camp. Just another bad guy.

I stood near his legs and nudged his mud-caked sneaker with the toe of my own shoe.

"Hey, Rafe Brooks, right?" When he didn't respond, I went on. "I'm Nell Massler. I'm here to save your life."

AFTER THAT KIND OF ANNOUNCEMENT, pretty much anything else I could say was going to be anti-climatic.

I knelt in the dirt by Rafe's head. His eyes were closed, but breath was definitely moving between his slightly parted lips. I wasn't sure where to touch him. Finally, I took hold of his shoulder and shook.

"Hey. Rafe. Come on, we have to get out of here." I glanced up at the cabin, unease filling me. Mallory Jones was supposed to be coming in from somewhere else, which meant she could show up any minute. I wanted to be as far away from this place as possible when that happened.

One eyelid drifted open, and he squinted at me, his gaze unfocused. "Who ..."

"Nell. I'm from—you might—damn. There's no time for this. We have to leave. Can you get up? I'm not sure I can move you by myself."

"I—" He moved his right arm, making as though to use his hand to push himself up. But as he did, his face contorted in pain, and he dropped again.

"Shit." My sense of urgency was practically screaming. I gritted my teeth and slid both hands beneath Rafe's chest and pulled. He tried to help, using the left arm as leverage and struggling to get to his knees.

"That's it. Great." I tried not to breathe too deeply as I shifted to raise him upward. "Can you put your good arm around me?"

He managed to sling it over my neck, and I grabbed his hand and stood. A dizzying sensation of zinging energy shot through me, but I didn't have time to consider what it was. Together Rafe and I lurched to the edge of the clearing and down the path.

"Where ... we ... going?" He breathed the words heavily into my ear.

"I saw cars down here. We have to get out of here fast."

He frowned, his brows drawing together, and blinked. "You don't have ... a way ... how did ..."

"I left my car on the road—God, we don't have time for explanations right now. I'm getting you out of here and once we're safe, you can play twenty questions all you want."

I could feel her coming. She was closer, and her power was palpable, so huge I could practically swim in it. I wished for the ability to fly or for super-strength to be able to throw Rafe over my shoulder and run to the car. But wishing didn't change anything, and it never had. So I just kept walking and dragging him with me.

"Where's everyone?" He was trying to turn his head and look behind us, but I only grunted and moved faster.

"Gone. For now. But not for long, so for the love of God, please move your ass."

We rounded a bend in the path, and at last I could see

the parking lot. I also spotted bodies pinned beneath trees, including the two men I'd thrown out of the way on my way in. If Rafe saw them, too, he didn't say anything.

The first car we reached had probably been silver at some point in time, but it was so rusted that I couldn't be completely sure of that. It was also locked. I could manage locks, but they were tricky for my telekinesis and took time—time we didn't have. I cursed under my breath and moved to the old black car I'd seen on my way in. It was open, and I leaned Rafe against the side before yanking the handle of the rear door. I maneuvered him into the back seat, trying not to drop him too hard, but judging by the sharp intake of breath, I didn't think I succeeded.

"Sorry." I leaned in and bent his legs at the knee so that I could shut the door and sprinted to the driver's seat, hoping that I could remember how to hot wire a car. I sagged in gratitude when I saw the keys were in the ignition. Why or how they were there, I didn't know, but I wasn't about to question any higher power that might be giving us a break.

When the engine turned over, part of me wanted to cry in relief. But we didn't have time for that kind of crap, even if I were the crying-in-relief kind of girl. I shifted the car into gear, backed to the center of the lot and floored the gas, sending us jostling along the narrow dirt road.

She was close, probably at the camp now. My heart pounded in time with the pulsating energy coming from her. Along with the dread, there was a tiny bit of fascination. The power to kill simply by glancing at someone ... what must that feel like? Could I learn to do that?

I shook my head, clearing it. That wasn't me, not now. A few years ago, maybe ... but not now. I wasn't the bad guy anymore. Today I was Nell the rescuer.

We got to the end of the dirt road, and I only paused a moment before I made a right, turning in the opposite direction of where my car was parked, on the chance that they might track me to it. I hit the gas again, and we careened away from the camp as fast as that car would go, driving toward the rising sun.

I'd looked at a map back in Florida, and I knew where we were heading, in a general sense, but for the first three hours, I simply drove. When we came to an intersection, sometimes I went straight and sometimes I made a random turn. About an hour and a half after we left the commune, I spied a sign for the interstate and headed in that direction, reasoning in the still-sensible part of my brain that being on a highway with other cars and people gave us a small measure of safety. I didn't think Mallory Jones and company were going to attack us in public. I hoped not.

Rafe was silent in the backseat. When I took a curve or a turn too hard, he groaned, but that was it. He wasn't asking questions or demanding explanations, and I wasn't sure if that was a good sign or a bad one.

The needle on the gas gauge was nudging 'E' when I finally felt it might be safe to pull off the road for a pit stop. I wasn't sure how accurate the gauge was, and running out of gas didn't seem to be a good option at this point. I found a busy exit and chose a gas station with several rows of pumps. Lots of people going through meant less chance of us being traced, I figured.

I used cash to fill the tank and buy us a couple of water bottles and a bag of chips. Nothing that might make us stand out from the throng of people passing, through. Since Rafe was alone in the locked car, I didn't linger in the store, but I did steal a minute to use the restroom.

He hadn't moved when I got back to the car. I climbed in and twisted in my seat to look down at him, make sure he was still breathing. As though he could feel my gaze, he opened his eyes.

"Do you need to use the bathroom while we're here? I want to keep going as long as we can once we're back on the road."

He closed his eyes again and shook his head. "I don't think I can move."

"I could help you. But this is probably not the place for that. And now that I think of it, you might be kind of ... you'd stand out in there. We don't want anyone to remember we were here."

"That's okay. I can take care of their minds. They wouldn't."

I had forgotten Rafe's ability. He was a manipulator, able to twist brains and memories. That put me on edge. I couldn't let him get to my own mind, not when I wasn't sure of his mental state.

"Still, there's a ton of people around here. You might miss one. Let's get a little further on and stop at a rest area. Oh, but here." I twisted open one of the water bottles and held it over the seat. "Are you thirsty?"

For a full minute, Rafe just stared at the bottle, as though he didn't realize what it was. And then he swiped it with his left hand, struggling to get it to his open mouth. I gritted my teeth, kicking myself. I had seen Cara tossing him down food and water yesterday, but how often did that happen? Why hadn't I thought sooner that he might need something to drink or eat?

"I'm sorry. I'm not a very good rescuer, I guess. I have some chips, too." I tore open the bag and set it on the floor in the backseat so that he could reach them. "That'll have to tide you over for now, until I can stop and get us something more. We need to get moving again."

"Where are we going?" His voice sounded a little stronger after the water, but he asked the question as though the answer didn't really matter to him.

"I'm not sure I should tell you exactly. I don't know what kind of trackers your friends at the camp have. Right now, I'm the only person who knows our destination. If they can focus on you, they might be able to figure it out. Like with a precog or something. But it's some place safe. Do you trust me?"

I didn't know where those last words had come from. I didn't care if Rafe trusted me or not; I had a job to do, and he was it.

His eyes met mine, flat and expressionless. "Does it matter? Do I have a choice?"

"Actually, no. You don't." I started the car and backed out. "But I'll tell you anyway. Keeping you safe is my assignment, and I'm one of those annoying people who always gets her own way."

"Are you from Carruthers? Did ... Cathryn send you?"

I glanced into the rearview as we merged back onto the

interstate. "Yes. Cathryn and Zoe. They're the only ones who knew I was coming for you." Which reminded me. I hadn't texted them. I had been so intent on getting away, it had slipped my mind.

Rafe was quiet for so long that I figured he had gone back to sleep or passed out again. Wrapped in my own worries, I jumped when he spoke.

"You should have left me there. They were going to finish me off this morning."

Frowning, I spared him a quick look. "Yeah, that's why I got you out of there. To miss out on the whole finishing-you-off deal. And also why I couldn't leave you there."

He coughed, a deep and wet sound that made me wonder if he might be sick. "If you're waiting for me to say thank you for saving my life, don't hold your breath. I'm already dead. You just got me away from them for a while."

"Bullshit. You don't know me, Rafe, but like I said, I always get what I want. And right now, for some reason, I don't want you dead. Of course, you keep talking like that and I might change my mind. I'm also not known for being a very nice person."

"I don't remember you from Carruthers. How do I know you're really ... part of them?" His breath was coming in short pants.

So he didn't know who I was. Either he hadn't heard me when I said my name back at the camp, or he was too traumatized to remember what the name Nell Massler meant in King. I decided that now wasn't the time to remind him.

"I haven't been working for them very long." I bit back a smile. That was an understatement. "I was um, activated especially for this mission. To rescue you. As for how you know I work for them, I can't prove it. Except I could tell you stuff about Cathryn and Zoe and Harper Creek that I wouldn't know if I hadn't been there and met them."

"Yeah, whatever. Doesn't matter who you are." His voice was scratchy again, and I heard the exhaustion, his words slurring a little as he drifted back to sleep. I focused on the road again.

When the signs for I-75 north appeared, I began watching for a rest area. Just past the intersection, I found one and pulled off the road. There weren't many people hanging around at that time of day, but I parked on the far side of the lot just to be safe, away from the older couple walking their poodle and the family stretching their own legs.

Rafe didn't move when the car stopped. I dug into my pocket and found the burner phone and switched it on. As Cathryn had said, there was one number in the contacts. I hit message and type in the three letters.

Yes

I held the phone in hands that weren't quite steady until I got back the confirmation that the message had been received. The temptation to send more—or to call and ask for instructions—was strong. I turned it off before I could act on that thought and climbed out of the car. With the door blocking me from the view of anyone who might be watching, I dropped the phone to the asphalt and stomped on it, one hard strike against the black plastic.

It splintered into several pieces. I scooped them up with care and shut the car door. A quick glance around assured me that no one was paying me any attention, and I slipped into the wooded area that bordered the rest rooms. A few pieces of the phone I scattered there, and then I tossed the rest in different directions, as far as I could fling them.

When I got back to the car, Rafe's eyes were open. I leaned inside.

"There's a bathroom here, and almost no one's around. I'll help you get to it."

I expected him to protest, but instead, he struggled to sit up, wincing. I noticed he was still protecting his right arm, holding it against his body when he sat. I opened his door and crouched to help him swing his legs out. He leaned on me, swaying a little as he got to his feet, but he didn't fall.

"It's right up here." I tried to affect a casual walk, as though I were just walking to the bathroom with my boyfriend's arm around my shoulders in affection, not because this guy couldn't quite make it there on his own. Rafe was leaning on me heavily, though, so I don't think I quite pulled it off.

"What happened to your arm?" I pointed to it as we reached the door to the bathrooms.

Rafe lifted a shoulder and then grimaced. "When the guy came to get me out of the hole this morning, he jumped in and landed on it."

I made a face, my imagination there with them in the ground. "Oh, my God. Is it broken?"

"I don't think so. Maybe. It doesn't matter." He pushed me away when I went to follow him into the men's room. "I got it from here."

"Don't be stupid. You can barely walk. If you pass out in that bathroom, it's going to be more trouble for me drag your ass back out. I'll close my eyes if it makes you feel better."

"No. I can do it. I only have to get the urinal." It was the first time he'd expressed a desire, and his face was determined, so I decided to take a chance. I backed away and held up my hands.

"Okay, big guy, go for it. If you end up face-down on the floor, give a yell and I'll come get you."

Rafe muttered something about the vote of confidence and moved into the bathroom, groping along the walls to hold him up as he went.

"Make sure you wash up when you're done. After you touch all that nastiness on the walls in there, I don't want your hands near me."

"Believe me, what's on these walls is nothing compared to what's already on me." His voice echoed out the door. A minute later, I heard his sigh of relief and the unmistakable sound of water hitting porcelain. I propped myself against the brick of the building and closed my eyes, casting my mind in a wide sweep to check for anyone with abilities near us. I came up empty except for Rafe, which made me breathe a little easier.

"Ready?" His voice at my side made me jump.

"God, you startled me." I pushed off the wall and stood near so that he could use me as a crutch. "Feel better?"

"I guess."

I had to bite my tongue and remember what Zoe had warned me. Rafe was at least as emotionally damaged as he was physically hurt, if not more so. The image of that grave alongside his own prison flashed across my mind, making me more gentle as I helped him into the back of the car.

"We're going to come up here and turn around." I met his eyes in the mirror. "I was hoping to throw off anyone who might be following us by stopping beyond the turnoff for the interstate and then doubling back."

"I thought I wasn't supposed to know where we're going."

"No, not until we get there. But I don't think this will hurt anything. I doubt they're reading your mind. Maybe just checking for intent."

"I know how to block. I blocked them the whole time we were in the camp. I have the guards up now."

"Cool. Me, too." I took the next exit and followed the ramp around and then back onto the highway in the opposite direction. "So don't try any of your mind bending with me. I know you think you don't want to be saved, but at some point you might be glad I did this."

He fell back against the seat, lying down again so that I couldn't see his face. "I doubt that. You have no idea."

"I know what happened. Or at least close enough."

"Then why didn't you let them just kill me? Get it over with?"

"Because." I eased up the pedal to keep us at the speed limit. No sense running afoul of some Georgia trooper with a speed gun. "Because it was my job. *Is* my job. And you might think your life is over, but you have people who don't agree. Like Cathryn and Zoe. And your grandparents."

I was pulling out the big guns, I knew, but he needed something to jolt him out of the pity party. He didn't answer right away.

"Do they know? What happened, I mean?"

I shrugged, though I knew he couldn't see me. "I'm not sure. But Cathryn will keep them up-to-date when she can. I know that."

He sighed, heavy and full of defeat. "I promised Gram.

But it didn't seem like a big deal then."

"Yeah, promises are bitches, aren't they?" When he didn't reply, I chanced a quick turn of my head to the backseat. His eyes were shut again, and his breathing was even. He was either sleeping or pretending to, and I decided to respect that. I needed some quiet myself, to figure out our next step.

Rafe slept solid for the rest of the trip, not even stirring when I stopped for gas at two different far-off-the-road gas stations. I was circling us closer to our real destination, but I couldn't risk buying a map, even at the podunk gas-and-go shops where I picked up food and other supplies a little bit at a time. Instead, I pulled into rest areas every few hours and stood in front of the huge laminated maps, studying them and trying to memorize the roads that would lead us to some rest.

"Witchcraft and telekinesis, my ass. What I need is a didactic memory."

If we had driven the direct route, I figured it would have taken us about seven hours to reach the safe house I'd chosen. Instead it was closing in on twelve hours of driving when I pulled off a tiny one-lane road and stopped the car on the shoulder.

"Are we there?"

I hadn't heard Rafe stir, but he was leaning toward me, propped on his one good arm.

"We're close to there. Actually, really close. Just up that hill." I pointed to the tree-covered mound next to the road.

"There isn't a road?" I might have mistaken Rafe's questions for curiosity if I hadn't seen the flat, dead expression in his dark eyes.

"Yeah, there's a road. But I'm not sure it's clear up there. If someone figured out where we were going, or if anyone's staying at the cabin right now ... I want to know. I was thinking of sneaking up and checking it out."

"Okay." Rafe swiveled his head to look out the window again, up the hill.

"But I don't want to leave you alone, either. So I thought maybe I could figure out another way to look around without leaving the car."

"You lost me." *And I don't really care*, said his tone. I ignored it and answered him.

"I can project. You know, like, be in two places at one time. Yesterday I went up to the camp to see where they were holding you, but my body never left Florida. No one could see me, either. You get it?"

"Yeah." His eyes narrowed. "You were at the camp yesterday?"

"I had to check it out and see where they were keeping you. Cathryn has been trying to get you out of there since— since things went bad. They sent in someone else a little while back, but it didn't go well for him. That's why they wanted me to recon first."

Pain flashed across Rafe's face, a hurt so deep and raw that I nearly reached out to touch him. He shut it down fast though, so I kept my hands to myself and started talking again to give him a minute.

"So I want to project up to the cabin and make sure everything is okay for us to go in. But I have a little problem.

When I've done this before, I needed either blood or some other kind of boost. I don't really feel like cutting myself here and maybe bleeding out, leaving you on your own."

I saw a hint of confused recollection in his eyes. Maybe Tasmyn had told him about me showing up in her dreams. If she had, it was only a matter of time before he put two and two together and figured out exactly who I was.

"What do you need, if not blood?" His voice was gruff.

"I'm not sure this will do the trick, but it might. I just need to touch you, draw a little of your energy to help me out. It worked yesterday with Cathryn and Zoe helping me. It's worth a try, at least."

"Sure. Whatever." He held out a hand, his non-hurting one. "This okay?"

"Uh-huh." I closed my eyes and sucked in a breath, ready for the dizzying vortex that had carried me to Georgia the day before. But when I touched Rafe's hand, there was no spinning. There was only power, raw and electric and mind-blowing, filling me and setting every nerve on fire. And right away, without even thinking about it, I was up at the cabin, precisely where I'd aimed to be. No pain, no nausea ... I was just *there*.

"Wow." I breathed out and glanced around. Not only had the trip been easier, but everything was so much crisper today than it had been when I'd projected to the camp. I didn't feel like I was walking in water when I moved. I stretched out my arms before me and stared. My virtual body was glowing, as though I were made up of millions of sparkling bits of light.

I didn't have time to sit and appreciate the sparkly glory that was me, though. Not now. The log cabin in front of me seemed empty and quiet, but anyone could be hiding inside. I crept over to a window and peered in, hoping that no one else could see glowy me.

Nothing was moving in the small living room. Sheets draped the furniture, but not even a breeze stirred them. I decided to take advantage of my invisibility and have a closer look.

Walking through walls in my projection state was something I'd never get used to doing. I grinned a little as I slipped through the door and moved around the cabin. Nothing and no one was hiding in the bedroom, the bathroom or the kitchen, and the living room was as empty as it had appeared, too. We would be safe here. For now, at least.

I almost didn't want to let go of the projection. I felt vibrant and alive, a buzz bordering on sensual. But Rafe needed me, and that was enough to remind me to let go. I closed my eyes and released my hold, willed my consciousness back to the car.

When I opened my eyes, Rafe was staring at me, a mix of awe and doubt in his expression. I released my hold on his hand and sat up.

"It looks okay up there. I think we'll be safe." I swiveled in the driver's seat to start up the car, but Rafe's hand on my shoulder made me freeze. That same jolt shot through me, but this time, with no intent to project, it just buzzed around my body, making me want to arch my back and moan. I held it together with the greatest of effort.

"What was that?" Rafe sounded more alive than he had in the last twelve hours, and that gave me a little hope. "Just now, when you went up there?"

"I told you, I project. My body stays put, but my consciousness—"

"No, I get that, but you ... your body here. You had this light all around you. Like you were on fire from the inside."

"Huh." I shook my head. "I don't know. That's never happened before. But my projection body was glowing. It was pretty cool." I turned around again, trying to ignore his fingers still touching me. I had my own theories about why his boost made me glitter girl, but sharing them right now was only going to bring up topics I wasn't ready to tackle yet. So I kept my mouth shut and drove us around the mountain to the cabin.

"What is this place? And where are we?" Rafe had stayed sitting up as we drove this time, and now he studied the log building, his eyes unreadable.

"We're in the mountains in Tennessee. Deep in the mountains. And this is a cabin that belongs to my family. Well, now to me. I haven't been here since I was a really little girl, so honestly, I wasn't even sure it was still here, but apparently it is."

"Does your family know you're here?"

I shook my head. "Nobody knows we're here. Cathryn and Zoe wouldn't let me tell them where I planned to take you, because it gave us a measure of security." I pulled the keys from the ignition and opened my door. "Wait here a minute. There's a generator in the back, or there used to be. Let me see if it's working. I'll be right back."

It was still there, and not only did it work, but there were several extra cans of gasoline, as if someone had expected us. I thanked whatever deity might be looking out for Rafe and me before I went back to the car.

"We're good on lights and power now. Come on, let's get you inside."

Rafe managed to push open the car door and swing his legs to the ground, but he was too weak to stand on his own. I hauled him to his feet, and together we shuffled up the steps of the porch.

"The door's locked, and I don't have a key. So give me a minute and let me see if I can open it my own way. If not, I'll have to break a window."

Rafe didn't answer, and I concentrated my focus on the lock, turning tumblers and then sliding the deadbolt. I was rewarded by a loud click, and the door swung inward.

"Nice." There might have been a hint of admiration in Rafe's voice, but I wasn't going to let it go to my head. I moved him inside, heading for the bedroom at first. I paused before we got there.

"Listen, I'm sure you just want to fall into bed at this point, but maybe it would be a good idea to clean you up first. I want to see if you have any injuries I need to treat before you pass out for the night, too. I picked up some medical supplies along our way. Nothing fancy, but if you have cuts or whatever ..."

Rafe shook his head and grimaced. "I'm okay. I don't need anything."

I rolled my eyes. "Look, buddy, if you think you're going to hide being sick or hurt from me and I'll just let it go, let you die in peace, you're wrong. I won't. I'm going to take you back to Carruthers whole and healthy eventually. If I have to tie you up to do it, I will. But for now, you're going to get cleaned up, and then I'm going to see what you need. We can do it the hard way. I'll strip you down and check every inch of your body. Or you can be adult about this and just tell me where it hurts."

He tensed, and I saw his jaw clench. For a minute, I thought I was going to have to make good on my threat. But then his body sagged against me. He didn't have the energy to fight.

"Fine. I don't have any cuts, I don't think. Doesn't feel like it. Something's wrong with my arm, but you knew that. I might have some broken ribs, because it hurts when I breathe sometimes. But mostly, it's just my head. I got some pretty hard hits. I probably had at least one concussion, from when I—when J—" His eyes closed. I stayed quiet and let him get through it.

"When Mallory was there. When she—it hit me, too. Knocked me out."

"Okay." I nodded and kept my voice neutral. "Not much we can do about the head, I think, other than keep you still and quiet while it gets better. I wish I could say I had the ability to heal, but I don't."

The faintest ghost of a smile skimmed over his lips. "You can leave your body, and you can pick locks with your mind. Don't underestimate the coolness factor there."

I raised one eyebrow. Whether he realized it or not, Rafe was still in there. A part of him was alive and kicking, in spite of his death wish.

"Let's get you to the bathroom, and I'll help you wash up." I walked us in that direction, but once we reached the door, Rafe pulled away from me.

"I can handle the shower. Just give me a towel."

"Are you sure? What if you pass out in there?"

He lifted a shoulder. "Then you can come in and drag

my body out, and check me all over for cuts and bruises, like you said. But I want to try to stay on my feet."

"Okay, fine. Suit yourself." I ducked under his arm into the bathroom and opened cabinets until I found a stack of towels. I pulled one out and laid on the vanity. "I can't promise how clean this is. I have no idea when people were last up here. But it looks all right." I sniffed it and nodded. "Yeah, it should work."

"Does it look like I'm going to complain? I've been in a hole in a ground for the last ..." He winced again and sagged against the wall. "I don't know how long I was there."

"It doesn't matter right now. Our priorities are getting you clean and into bed, and then tomorrow, if you're feeling up to it, we can talk about ... other stuff."

He didn't answer me as he closed the door. I waited, listening for the water to go on, and then something occurred to me.

"Rafe, hold on a minute. I probably have to turn the water on from outside. I remember this place was on a well, because my grandfather took me out with him to get it set up, once. Let me see if I can remember where the valve is."

I opened a kitchen drawer and smiled that the flashlight was where I remembered it should be. And happily, the water valve was also easily found. By the time I got back inside, I could hear the shower running.

I knocked lightly on the bathroom door. "You doing okay in there?"

"Yeah." Rafe's voice was muffled and a little strained, but at least he was talking. "I'm good."

I chanced leaving him alone to finish up and went to the

bedroom to fold down the covers. The sheets smelled a little musty, but they would work for tonight. I found an extra blanket in the closet and laid it over the bedspread. It was June, but up here in the mountains, nights were still chilly.

"Hey!" Rafe yelled, and I sprinted back to the bathroom, my heart pounding. Had he fallen, or did someone come in ... ?

"Yes—I'm here. Are you okay?"

"Yeah, I'm fine." The water had turned off, I noted. He must have been out of the shower. "But now that I'm clean, I don't want to put these clothes back on. You have anything I can wear for now?"

Shit. I didn't. I hadn't shopped for clothes along the way, and it hadn't even occurred to me that we were both going to need some. I could make a trip down the mountain, find a store in a few days, but that wasn't going to help us tonight.

"I don't have extra clothes. There might be something left over in the cabin, but mostly it was women here." I racked my brain and then went back to the bedroom and found a folded sheet in the chest at the end of the bed.

Rafe had cracked the door open when I returned, and steam escaped. I had a quick view of him wearing nothing but the towel around his waist, water dotting his chest and stomach. He was painfully thin. The bones in his shoulders stood out, and I could nearly count his ribs. But damn, still ...

He was using a smaller towel to dry his hair. He had worn it short in the pictures I'd seen in his files, but now it was skimming the top of his shoulders. I supposed that made sense; the people who threw him in a hole in the ground and barely kept him alive weren't going to haul him up for a weekly shave and haircut. A scruff of beard covered his cheeks and chin. I hadn't noticed before, thanks to the layer of dirt and filth.

He caught me staring at him and cocked his head.

"Something to wear?"

"Oh, uh, I'll have to look later. But for now, just wrap yourself in this." I thrust the sheet into the bathroom.

Rafe took it and held it for a moment without speaking. He shut the door, and I heard him fumbling, cursing a little under his breath.

"I'm sorry," I called through the door. "I'll get us some clothes as soon as I can. We just have to make do for tonight. Okay?"

The door swung open again. Rafe had draped the sheet around his waist and up over his shoulders, almost like a toga. He clutched the extra in his good hand. I bit my lips to hide a smile.

"Well, you smell much better." I offered my shoulder. He laid his bare arm around my neck and when it touched my skin, that same fissure of energy struck. I gasped in spite of myself, and for a breath of time, I wasn't certain if I was going to jump away or pull him closer.

"What?" He stared down at me, suspicious.

"Nothing. Just your arm was cold against my neck." It was a bald-face lie, since his skin was still warm from the shower, but he didn't call me on it. Exhaustion had settled in lines on his face, and when we got the bedroom, he didn't fight me as I helped him into the bed.

"There's no central heat, but I'll try to get a fire going, so we'll leave your door open. That way if you need anything, you can call and I'll hear you."

I moved to the doorway before Rafe called.

"Hey. I realized when I was in the bathroom—I don't know your name."

I paused before turning, plastering a smile on my face. I wasn't dealing with this tonight.

"You mean to tell me I saved your ass today, dragged you out of perdition and half way around the country, and you don't even know what to call me?" I shook my head. "Go to sleep, Rafe. We'll talk in the morning."

I walked out of the room fast, but he didn't call me back. A few minutes went by, as I stood waiting in the center of the living room, and then the bedside light went off. I breathed a sigh of relief.

Telling Rafe who I was could definitely wait until tomorrow. Tonight ... I needed sleep. Everything that had happened today caught up with me all of a sudden. I pulled the dusty white sheet away from the couch, kicked off my shoes and sank down. Oblivion followed, and I didn't open my eyes for a long time.

CHAPTER 9

IT WAS THE BIRDS that woke me in the morning, chirping all too happily in the dappled sunlight. I blinked, disoriented. This wasn't the hospital, and yet it felt familiar ... The day before came rushing back to me, and I sat up, my heart thumping and my mind on instant alert. I'd been passed out, so exhausted that anyone could have snuck up on us and I wouldn't have heard. I cast my mind around, as far as I could, but I didn't pick up a single blip of power. I sagged back in relief.

The air was cool, and I kicked myself for falling asleep before I had the chance to make a fire. Rafe might have been freezing. I hopped up and tiptoed to the door of the bedroom, but he was still asleep, the covers moving up and down in a reassuring rhythm.

It didn't take long to find the woodpile and build up a good blaze. Once it was going, I brought in the bags of food I'd left in the car overnight and put everything away. There wasn't much, but it would see us through until it was safe for me to make a trip to the nearest town for groceries.

I took advantage of Rafe's silence and showered. His clothes from the day before were still on the bathroom floor, rolled up in a ball. I tossed them out into the hallway along with my own clothes. I'd found a drawer full of women's clothing, and while most of it was too big for me, it would do while I washed everything else.

Clean, with a towel wrapped around my hair and wearing an oversized skirt and t-shirt, I picked up the pile of dirty clothes and went out to the washing machine in the lean-to. Some wonderful person had left a bottle of detergent, and I dumped everything in, along with our towels.

When I went back inside, there was a different vibe, and I knew Rafe was awake. I stuck my head in the bedroom door.

"So, how are you feeling?"

He stirred, his eyes meeting mine. "Okay, I guess."

"Sorry if you got cold last night. I was more tired than I thought, and I passed out without getting a fire going. It's good now, though. And it'll probably be warmer today. Are you hungry?"

He made a noise I couldn't interpret. "I could eat."

"Great. I can't cook at all, but there's some bread. And peanut butter. Oh, and some jelly, too."

Rafe shook his head. "Whatever. Could I get some water?"

"Sure." I pulled a water bottle from the fridge and brought it back, studying him as I approached the bed. He looked a little less tired; his eyes were not quite as shadowed. I unscrewed the lid of the bottle and handed it to him.

"Thanks ... ummm ..." He took a swig, eyes closed, and then set the bottle on the night table. "So are you going to tell me your name? You never did last night."

"No, I didn't." I sat on the edge of the bed near his feet. "I did say it, though, when I first saw you yesterday. You must have just forgotten, in all the-running-for-our-lives. Not to mention the passing out and driving for freaking ever. Or maybe when we shared energy so I could project." I was babbling, saying anything to keep from answering his question about my name.

"Yeah, that was wild." Rafe pushed himself to a sitting position, maneuvering the pillows behind his back. "What was it?"

"I don't know for sure." I clasped my hands around my knees. "Like I said, that was new. I always used blood for projecting before, and then yesterday, Cathryn and Zoe helped me. Zoe called it boosting my power. But it wasn't like with you, with the glowing ... and everything was much clearer yesterday, too. The only thing I can think is that because we're both from First Families, there might be some deeper connection."

Absorbed in my theory, I didn't pay attention to what I was saying until I saw the look of confusion on Rafe's face. *Shit.*

"What's your name?" His voice was quiet, almost deadly calm.

"Nell Massler." There wasn't any sense in prevaricating. He had to find out at some point. I never cared what anyone thought of me, ever, but somehow, now, Rafe's opinion of me mattered. A lot.

Recognition and recollection dawned in his eyes, and he recoiled from me. "Nell Massler? As in, the witch who tried to kill Tasmyn? From King? What the *fuck*?"

He was struggling to get out of bed, to get away from me, and I closed my eyes, fighting back the anger and the power that wanted lash out and show him who Nell Massler really was.

"Rafe, calm down. I can imagine what you've heard about me, but I'm really only here to help you. I do work for Carruthers. I didn't lie about anything."

"You didn't tell me you were Nell-fucking-Massler. You're supposed to be in a mental hospital. Away from people."

They hurt, the words did, probably more than they should have. After all, he only spoke the truth. But hearing them from his mouth was hard.

"I was. And then I was in a coma for over a year. But Cathryn and Zoe woke me up to save your life."

"Coma?" His eyes narrowed. "Why were you in a coma?"

I looked over his shoulder at the pillow. "I had to do something, and it took more out of me than I had thought. I guess I needed the rest."

"What did you have to do? Were you trying to hurt Tas again?"

"No! For God's sake, no. I wanted to help her. I projected to Marica's house that last day. It was an involved process, and it knocked me out. For a year. Well, a little more than that."

He stared at me. "That's the truth?"

"It is." I stood up. "And when Cathryn needed someone she could count on to save your life, she woke me up and here I am. Here we are. Now, unless you have any more questions, I'm going to go make your breakfast."

I stalked out of the bedroom with what was left of my dignity. What did it matter what Rafe Brooks thought of me? He was a job, nothing more. He could hate me to hell and back as far as I cared.

I slapped a knife full of peanut butter and a spoonful of jelly on two pieces of bread, put them together and slammed the concoction onto a plate. When I got back into the bedroom, I dropped it onto Rafe's lap.

"Bon appetite." I wheeled back around.

"Nell? Hey, wait a minute."

I stopped in the doorway, but I didn't face him again.

"I didn't mean to jump to conclusions about you. I don't know who you are, really. I heard stuff from Tasmyn and Amber—oh, and Cara, too. But you got me out of the camp, and if you say you work for Carruthers, I have to believe you."

"Believe me or not, I don't care. My job is to keep you alive and get you back to Harper Creek. You don't have to like me or trust me for that to happen. But you need to do what I say. So eat up."

I left before he could say anything else, slamming the cabin door behind me and heading for the washing machine. The clothes were finished, and I found a bag of clothespins on the line. I pinned them up and stomped back into the house.

Taking advantage of my indignation-fueled energy, I ripped the sheets off the rest of the furniture and carried them all outside to wash. When I went inside again, I found the tote of cleaning supplies and tackled the kitchen and the bathroom, scrubbing and mopping until everything smelled fresh and clean.

I'd never cleaned, done laundry or cooked a day in my life, yet today I'd done all three. Well, if making a peanut butter sandwich counted as cooking, which in my world, it absolutely did. Yeah, Nell Massler was turning over a new leaf.

I avoided Rafe's room until nearly two o'clock, when I began to feel guilty for ignoring him. I stuck my head in the bedroom.

"Hey, you hungry again? I have a couple of cans of soup I think I can manage to not burn."

Rafe stirred under the covers, but he didn't answer. I stepped inside, noting the crumb-covered plate and empty water bottle sitting on the night stand.

"Rafe? You sleeping?" Yeah, a dumb question, as he lay there, not answering me.

"Hey." I reached out to shake his shoulder, bare where the sheet had ridden down. But when I touched his skin, it radiated heat, more than just the shock of power I'd felt before. He was burning up. I tugged the comforter away from his face, and my heart plummeted when I saw it was flushed.

"Shit. Shit, shit, shit. Rafe." I did shake him this time, and he blinked at me, his eyes glazed and unfocused.

"Joss?" He mumbled her name, and I dropped my hand and stepped back. He shifted again, rolling to his back. I could hear the rattle in his chest and see the shuddering effort of his breath.

"Oh my God, Rafe." I ran my hands back over my hair, pulling it as I tried to think. It must be pneumonia. Didn't people with pneumonia have high fevers and sound like they couldn't breathe? Rafe had mentioned some broken ribs, but those wouldn't cause symptoms like he was having. Unless they punctured his lung. Which would have happened earlier, and he would have noticed. I thought, anyway.

I ran back to the living room and dug out the bag that held the medical supplies I'd bought yesterday. There was a bottle of ibuprofen, and I knew that would help with fever if I could get him to take it. Other than that ... nothing. I was fairly certain pneumonia required antibiotics, and strangely enough, they didn't sell those at gas station mini-marts.

I took a deep breath and calmed my mind. First things first. I took a bottle of water from the fridge and carried it, along with three ibuprofen, into the bedroom.

"Rafe, you've got to sit up. Come on now, just a little bit." I slid my hand under his back, blanching at the heat there. Rafe moaned again and fought me as I tried to lift him.

"Rafe. You have to take this medicine. Open your eyes and sit up just a little, or so help me ..." I couldn't think of a threat strong enough. What was I going to do, call his grandmother? I didn't even have a phone.

His eyes half-opened, and I held the bottle in front of his face. "See? Water. Time to have a drink."

His lips parted a little, and I took advantage of that to stick the pills into his mouth. I held the rim of the bottle to his lips and poured it in.

"Swallow. Come on, Rafe. Swallow the water."

He did finally, drinking it down in three large gulps. I lay him back down and recapped the bottle.

"Joss." He spoke again, this time his eyes seeking me out. "Please." The pleading in his voice almost broke my heart. "Don't go. I'll take care of you. Don't ..." He ended on a half-sob, and I couldn't help myself. I sat down on the edge of bed, right next to him, and I touched his cheek with my palm, steeling myself for the flare.

"It's all right, Rafe. You're going to be okay. I won't leave you." I kept my tone low and reassuring. With one last shudder, he sank back into the pillow and subsided. I was about to stand up again when his hand came up and covered mine on his cheek. He murmured something and turned his face to press his lips into my palm. A new sensation sizzled up my arm. It was as strong as the other buzz I'd felt when touching Rafe, but there was an added component of ... sweetness. Something nearly unfamiliar to me, and yet I remembered the feeling.

He thinks I'm Joss, I reminded myself, and then had to ask why that mattered. I had a job to do, and keeping Rafe alive was it. Throwing my little temper snit this morning and ignoring him may have cost me valuable time in doing that job. If I had checked on him sooner ... maybe ...

I eased my hand away, and this time, Rafe let it go. He rolled to his side again and seemed to sink deeper into sleep.

The way I figured it, I had two battles to fight. I had to try to bring down his fever, and I had to make sure he could breathe easily. I didn't really know how I could do either of those things, other than keep him hydrated and give him more ibuprofen. My medical training was non-existent. I only knew what I'd seen on television or read in books.

Which reminded me. Didn't they sometimes put feverish patients into a bath? I couldn't manage that with Rafe, but ...

I went back to the kitchen, found a basket of rags and soaked them in cold water. I put them into a bowl and carried them into the bedroom, wringing one out before I positioned it over Rafe's forehead.

It was so hot, I nearly expected to hear a sizzle, but he didn't even flinch as the cold water hit his skin. I went back to the living room to pace and think.

If only I had a computer, or a phone, or anything that would let me access the internet. I could look up how to take care of someone with pneumonia. Or I'd call Cathryn and ask her what to do. But no, here we were, out in the middle of fucking nowhere, with no one to help.

The rest of the afternoon and evening passed in a blur for me. I alternated between sitting at Rafe's bedside, changing out the cool cloths on his forehead and forcing water down his throat whenever his eyes opened, and stalking back and forth across the living room floor, wracking my brain for anything that might help him.

The later it became, the worse Rafe seemed to get. I vaguely remembered hearing once that fevers tended to get worse at night. I couldn't remember why, any more than I could remember what to do to make them go away. I dosed him with more fever reducer at eight o'clock, and sometime between then and eleven, I fell asleep, leaning over him on the bed.

He was muttering in his sleep again, which was what awoke me. This time, it wasn't Joss; he was arguing with Tasmyn, talking about Marica and railing at her about something I couldn't understand.

"Another trip down memory lane with Rafe's old girlfriends." I sighed and rubbed the back of my neck where it was stiff from my sleeping position. The cloth had slipped from his head, and it was warm again, anyway. I replaced it with a new one and stood to stretch.

The bed began to shake as Rafe was abruptly struck with

a chill, his body shivering as he tried to draw his arms and legs in as tight as possible. I cursed and took away the cool cloth, wondering if that had kicked off this new symptom or if it were just another manifestation of the fever itself.

He didn't seem to be able to get warm. In desperation, I climbed into the bed with him and plastered my body to his, pulling the covers up over us both to make as much heat as possible. That seemed to work, as he stopped shaking and relaxed a little more. I closed my eyes, and I came as close to praying for help as I had in a long time.

Rafe and I both spent a fitful night. I dosed him with meds every four hours, and I wiped down his face with cold water each time. I managed to make him drink another bottle of water. But the fever just kept coming back, and I was afraid his breathing was worse.

He had another attack of chills in the early morning light, and I climbed under the covers with him again. When I opened my eyes, the living room was full of sunshine. I knew it had to be nearly mid-morning.

I left Rafe sleeping in relative peace and went to use the bathroom, wash my face and wander helplessly around the small cabin. I caught sight of yesterday's laundry, still on the clothes line blowing in the wind. I had never taken it in. A quick glance at Rafe told me he was asleep, so I ran outside to take down the clothes and bring them inside.

I carried Rafe's clean t-shirt and jeans into the bedroom and was just laying them in a dresser drawer when I heard a sound behind me. Rafe had rolled to his back, and his breath was coming in such short puffs and with such struggle that the entire bed was shaking.

I stood, staring at him, trying so hard to breathe. This same boy, this guy I'd seen in person for the first time only the day before, who didn't want to live anymore, was fighting damn hard to hold onto life. His mouth was open and his head thrown back, as though the air he sought was just a little bit above his reach.

There was nothing I could do to help him. I wanted to scream, and I wanted to hit something. Possibly someone. Had I rescued Rafe from that camp only to watch him die up here in the mountains? And it would be a more horrific death than Mallory Jones' quick strike would have been, I was sure. If I knew there was a doctor somewhere around here, I'd take him in, but I had no idea where the nearest practice was. It could have been hours away, and driving Rafe that far was impossible at this point.

I couldn't bear to watch him suffer. I turned on my heel and opened the front door. I stood for a moment on the porch, staring into the trees and wishing for an answer, any answer at all.

"Well, hey there, young lady! I haven't seen anyone in this old place for a long time."

It felt as though I jumped a foot in the air. My heart thumped wildly, and my hands clenched the porch rail. I glanced around for any possible weapon, but the old man who approached me didn't seem threatening. The smile he wore was downright brilliant.

"Sorry, didn't mean to startle you. I was taking my daily walk, and I always cut across here, by this property. I'd ask the owners if it were okay, but like I said, the cabin always sits empty. Until today." He wasn't very tall, and his hair was totally white. He wore it a little longer than most men his age, brushing the top of his shoulders. His face was a map of wrinkles, but his eyes were kind.

"Yeah, we just got in ... last night." I watched the man carefully. He checked out as not possessing any powers, although I got a weird sort of feeling from him. He wasn't exactly blocking me, but I couldn't get a sense of him. There was simply a lovely calm, just what I needed in the middle of my current freak-out.

"That's just fine, isn't it. A little vacation, huh?"

"I guess you might say that." I stood stiff, not trusting myself to move.

"I took a vacation just once in my life, before I retired, that is. Me and the wife went to Nashville, so she could see her favorite singers there. She was a little star-struck, for sure. She would have gone back every year, if I'd let her. Of course, a doctor's life doesn't give him much chance for vacations."

His words knocked around my brain for a few seconds before they sunk in. And then I practically screamed at the poor man.

"Doctor? You're a doctor?" I leaned across the railing. "My friend who's here with me is really, really sick. I think he has pneumonia. I've been trying to keep him comfortable, get the fever down, but I'm pretty sure he's getting worse. I don't know any place to take him to see a doctor or go to a hospital, but even if I did, I don't think he'd make it." I met his blue eyes with mine. "Please, do you have antibiotics you could give him? Or anything else I could do to help him?"

The man studied me, his face lined with compassion. "I don't have any medicine like that, for sure. I'm sorry. But honey, I've been treating people since a long time back, and I've beat more cases of pneumonia than most doctors see in a lifetime. It might be that I could help you out. Mind if I take a look at the patient?"

For the length of a heartbeat, I hesitated, and then I nodded. "Sure. He's in the bedroom. Come on in." If this man turned out to be a spy for Mallory Jones' group, the worst he was going to do was kill Rafe and then me. Rafe was already headed that way, I was afraid, and if he didn't make it, I was thinking I didn't want to, either. So we had nothing to lose.

The man climbed the porch, breathing hard and muttering about old bones and creaking bodies.

"I don't suppose you're any relation to the Bradors, are you? They're the family who own this place, or they did."

I nodded. "I'm related. That was—they were—or are, I guess, my mother's family."

"Ah, fine, fine." He allowed me to lead him into the bedroom, and I stepped aside. "This is Rafe. He started with the fever yesterday morning, and it got bad fast. The chills began last night, and then this thing with his breathing ..."

The doctor looked down at Rafe, his head tilted. He took hold of his wrist, taking his pulse, I supposed, and then he knelt down on the floor and laid his ear against the heaving chest. I watched as he moved his ear from spot to spot, his expression grave.

Finally he rose. "I'd have to say you're right, young lady. Sounds like pneumonia to me. Pretty bad case, too." He saw my face and hastened on. "But don't you fret. I told you, I beat pneumonia. I have some medicines, some natural remedies that should help ease his breathing and make him more comfortable. I live just the next cabin over the hill, so I'll run home and get what we need."

I thought for a minute. "I have a car. You can use it, if it'll be faster."

He shook his head. "No, as these hills go, the way the crow flies is the best way to get around. I have a path that leads up to my front door. You just sit put for a minute and I'll be back." He began walking out but stopped and stood before me.

"By the way, I'm Eli Alva. Folks here just call me Dr. Eli, or Doc." He stuck out a hand.

I took his hand, grateful for the firm grip. "I'm Nell. Nice to meet you, Dr. Eli."

CHAPTER
10

OVER THE NEXT TWELVE hours, I worked harder than I ever had in my life, just to keep Rafe Brooks alive.

Doc was as good as his word. He made it back with amazing alacrity, carrying an old-fashioned black medical bag. He laid it on the kitchen table and began removing things from it.

First there was a burlap bag full of onions. And then he pulled out a handful of bright orange flowers, complete with the roots attached. Next came a clutch of odd-looking tubular dried flowers. I was beginning to have my doubts; was this old man out of his mind?

"Don't go panicking, Nell dear. I promise these all make sense." He picked up the bag of onions. "If you would, cut the onions up in slices and set them to cooking a bit. We're going to need them for a poultice."

I had no earthly idea what a poultice might be, but if it would help Rafe, I would cut onions until my eyes fell out.

Dr. Eli took out a pouch and held it up to me. "Can you put on the kettle as well, please? I brought the pleurisy root dried, but I also picked some fresh from my garden, so you could see what I'm using. This is one of our best remedies against lung ailments. We need to put a teaspoonful into a cup of boiling water and make the patient drink it once an hour."

I raised my eyebrows. "Good luck with that. I've barely been able to get him to drink water."

The doctor chuckled. "My dear, I've wrangled patients much more wily than your young man. Forty years of practice. I've seen it all."

"Hmm." I set water to heat and went back to cutting the onions. I was butchering them, but then again, aesthetics hardly counted in this situation. "So what's the dried tube looking thing?"

Doc crushed them in his hand. "This is Baikal Skullcap. Chinese herb, so I can't grow it here, but I buy it. We'll combine it with the goldenseal, and it should help our boy in there."

I finished cutting the onions and followed the doctor's instructions for cooking them, letting them steam until they were soft. He showed me how to carefully wrap the onions in a square of cheesecloth he'd brought, and we carried it, along with the cup of pleurisy root tea, into the bedroom.

Somehow, Doc got the hot tea down Rafe's throat and then dosed him with the goldenseal and Baikal Skullcap. Once our patient was lying down again, Doc helped me settle the poultice on his chest and then cover him carefully.

"What now?" I stood next to the bed, my arms crossed as I watched Rafe closely for signs of improvement.

"Now, we wait. We let the medicines do their work. And we might want to make up a second poultice, so that we can alternate them as needed."

Under Doc's eyes, waiting was not a spectator sport. Each time I'd think I had done everything he asked, there would be one more task. One more set of dishes to wash.

"Build up that fire, would you?" he called. "And if you have any more blankets, heat them in front of it and then bring them in. He's about to have another attack of chills."

After the fourth dose of the pleurisy root tea, Rafe began to cough, deep and loud. I ran into the bedroom in alarm and held my hand to my mouth as he choked and gagged. But Dr. Eli wasn't alarmed. He leaned over Rafe, holding beneath the patient's mouth a bowl he'd asked me to bring him a few minutes before.

"That's it, boy, get it out. Spit it out." And on command, Rafe did. After a few coughing fits like that, he settled back down into what seemed to be a more peaceful sleep, with his chest no longer heaving and his breathing more even.

A couple of hours later, I brought in a reheated poultice. I was removing the old one and centering the new when I noticed beaded moisture on Rafe's forehead and upper lip.

"Doc, he's sweating. What's happening now?" I wrung my hands; just when I thought he was maybe getting better, now there was a brand new symptom.

Dr. Eli only smiled at me, his hands resting on his stomach as he leaned back in the chair.

"It means his fever's broke. That's good news, very good news."

I sank into the chair the doctor had pulled up next to the bed for me a few hours before. "Really? So you think he's going to make it?"

He nodded. "I think he is. Now, mind you, he's going to

need rest, and likely it will take a week or two before he's back on his feet. But you kept him alive, and that's no little thing, Miss Nell."

I shook my head. "No, Doc, *you* kept him alive. If you hadn't come down that path right then, I don't know what I would have done. I didn't know any of that stuff."

"Well, I had the knowledge, and you did the hard work. I'd say we made a pretty decent team." He stood then, his hand on his back. "But this old body isn't used to sleeping in bedside chairs any more. Once upon a time, seemed like that was the only place I got sleep, but now I'm accustomed to the soft life. I like my bed."

I stood up, too, and laid a hand on the old man's arm. "Let me drive you home. It's got to be after midnight. You can't walk the path in the dark."

"Can and will, my dear. I've been sneaking around these mountains in the dark and in the light for many a year. Besides, if your young man wakes up, I don't want him alone. He might try to do something stupid, and you need to keep him quiet. Understand?"

I nodded. "Okay. If you're sure. Oh, and please apologize to your wife for me, for keeping you out so long. She must be worried."

His face softened. "Oh, child, I lost my Nancy Rose nearly ten years ago. She's beyond the worrying point now. But thank you for that." He reached out and touched my face with just one wizened finger. "She would have liked you. She favored spunky girls, and Nell, dear, you have spunk in spades."

I smiled, but for some reason I couldn't explain, tears filled my eyes. Crap, was I becoming one of those girly girls who cried at card commercials?

"I don't feel very spunky right now. I think I could sleep for a week."

Doc led me out to the kitchen and began to gather things back into his bag. "And you might just do that, but it doesn't mean that you're any less for it." He pushed the remaining onions across the table. "I'm going to leave these with you, in case he needs another poultice, but I think you're going to be okay with what you have. He'll only need it another couple of hours, then you can stop that." He touched the packet of Baikal Skullcap and goldenseal, and then the bowl of dried pleurisy root. "Keep dosing him with the Skullcap mix and the tea, at least a few days. As long as you can make him take it, I'd say. Once he's strong enough to fight you hard about the medicines, we'll know he's past the point of needing them."

"Okay." I nodded. "Anything else I should know?"

"Just keep him hydrated and watch him when he needs to get up to use the bathroom. He'll be weak as a newborn kitten for a while. You don't want him falling down and hitting his head."

No, we didn't need another concussion, I thought. But aloud I only said, "Got it. Is that it?"

"Pretty much. I'll come by to check on him in a few days, but in the meantime, if something were to go seriously amiss, just scamper down the path there. You'll find me eventually."

"Thank you, Doc. I know it sounds like such a little thing to say, but thank you. You saved Rafe's life tonight. I'll never forget it. Or you."

He stood for a moment, staring at me with an odd

expression on his face. I realized it was similar to what I'd seen in Zoe's eyes before, which was surprising, since there was nothing else like her in this old country doctor.

And then he stepped toward me, his arms open. For some reason I would never have been able to explain, I let him pull me into a hug. Me, the girl who didn't do hugs, not ever. Now in only a few days, I'd let Zoe and Doc put their arms around me. I was going soft.

"I can tell by looking at you that you're tough, Nell Massler. So life has thrown some junk at you to make you that way. That's okay. Tough is good. Tough gets you through the messy parts of life. Tough saves people. But you're not hard, and don't forget that. Being hard makes your heart shrivel up, and that's not you. No one with a shriveled heart would have worked like you did to save that boy's life."

He clapped me once on the back and then stepped away, picking up his bag. I didn't say anything as he whistled out the door, closing it behind him with quiet precision.

Rafe was still breathing easy when I went back into the bedroom. His face and chest were now covered in perspiration, and I wiped him down with a dry towel. Once I was sure he was quiet and comfortable, I gave into the utter exhaustion and fell onto the bed next to him, my eyes closed before my head even hit the pillow.

CHAPTER
11

"NELL. HEY, NELL."

I pushed back against the finger that was poking into my shoulder. "No. Not yet. Sleep. So tired."

"Nell. C'mon, wake up. Please."

It was the *please* and the urgent tone that finally drilled through my sleepy haze. I blinked up into Rafe's dark eyes, and I was instantly awake.

"What? What's wrong? Are you okay?"

He nodded, his head scratching against the pillow. "I think so. But I need to use the bathroom, and I can't get my legs to move. I'm sorry to wake you up, but can you help?"

I pushed myself to a sitting position and ran a hand over my hair. "Yeah, hold on just a second." I swung my legs over the side of the bed and glanced out to the living room. It was filled with bright sunshine, which told me we'd both slept away most of the morning. That was a good thing, probably. We needed it.

I helped Rafe up and wrapped the sheet around his waist, holding it for him so he could lean on me. He was weaker than he'd been the day we arrived, but given that he'd just cheated death again, that was hardly surprising. He shuffled his feet as we moved toward the door.

"What the hell happened?" His voice was scratchy again, and I made a mental note to get more water into him as soon as he was finished in the bathroom.

"Well, Rafe, you tried to die on me again." I worked hard to keep the wobble out of my own words. "I really would appreciate it if you stopped doing that. It kind of gets on my nerves."

His brow knitted, and his lips were tight with the concentration of getting across to the bathroom. "What are you talking about?"

"Pneumonia, Rafe. You had pneumonia. I came in from my tantrum, and you were delirious with fever. I couldn't get it to come down, and then you were struggling to breathe." I wiped away the picture of him from the day before, his chest heaving up and down as he tried to get air. It wasn't a memory I wanted to keep.

He swung away from me, propped against the wall, and shuffled into the bathroom on his own. "And you didn't let me die. Again."

Before I could say anything to that, he closed the door between us. I didn't bother fighting him on going in by himself. Worst case, I knew now I could drag him back to bed if I had to.

When he finished and opened the door again, I stepped up without a word. Rafe took hold of my shoulder and leaned on me. We had to stop once when a coughing fit took hold of him, but I got him back into bed. He pushed the pillows up and sat against them.

"What's this?" He held up the onion-soaked square of cheesecloth, frowning.

"It's an onion poultice." I said it as though any idiot would know that.

"And that is ... ?"

"One of the things that saved your life. Which reminds me." I went back to the kitchen and got a bottle of water and thrust it in Rafe's face. "Here. Drink up. You need to stay hydrated. I'm going to make you some more medicine, and I'll be right back with it."

I brewed the tea and brought the powdered Skullcap in with me. Rafe eyed me skeptically.

"Are you sure you know what you're doing?"

I ignored the implied criticism. "I do. Here, drink this."

"What is it?"

"Brewed pleurisy root." I held out the cup.

Rafe sniffed it and made a face. "No, thanks."

"Damn it, Rafe, drink it and shut up. Or I will pin you on the bed and pour it down your throat." He was pissing me off with this attitude.

His eyes narrowed. "I'm not going to do it."

"Really?" I put my hands on my hips and focused on him. It wasn't hard to force his hands down to the mattress, where they fisted at his side. I kept the pressure up, and then stepping closer to the bed, I worked on gently prying his lips apart with my mind, used my free hand to tilt back his head and trickled the tea down his ungrateful throat.

He gagged just a little, but most of it went down. I made sure he swallowed before I released him from my mental grip.

"God damn it, what's wrong with you?" Rafe was

furious, but he was also too weak to do anything about it. I favored him with a sweet smile.

"Right now, not one blessed thing. I'll give you a break on the Skullcap for now, but you're going to take it. You might as well just do it the easy way next time."

I walked out of the bedroom, grinning. Who knew being a nurse could be so much fun?

I peeked in at Rafe thirty minutes later. He was asleep again, but when I chanced a light touch to his forehead, it was still blessedly cool. I left him napping and went out to sit on the porch. The sun was shining and warm, but there was just enough of a breeze to make it a perfect day. Sitting on the swinging bench, with the buzzing of bees and chirping of birds, with no trace of any extraordinary people around other than myself and my patient, life felt pretty damn good.

I went back inside after an hour or so. Rafe had had long enough a reprieve. I brewed another cup of tea and took out a bottle of water, adding the tincture of goldenseal and Skullcap to it and shaking well.

Rafe was awake when I went back in. He scowled at me with distrust.

"Did you have a nice nap?" I kept my voice light and tried to make my face pleasant as possible.

"Yeah." He coughed, his whole body shaking with the effort, but even then, he sounded better than he had twenty-four hours before.

"Excellent. Time for your next dose. And don't worry, you only have to take it a little while longer."

He sighed. "Just where did you get this stuff? Do you always travel with this witch doctor crap?"

It was taking all of my very-low reserve of restraint not

to lose my temper. "No, if you must know. All I had was ibuprofen, and it wasn't doing shit for you or your fever. I was at the point yesterday where I couldn't do anything else. I thought you were going to die. And then this old man came up the path outside ... he was a doctor. Retired, but still. And he's practiced here in the mountains his whole life, so he knew what would make you better."

I stuck out my hand with the mug of pleurisy root tea. Rafe, distracted by what I was saying about the doctor, took it without thinking and drank. I hid my smile.

"So you let a stranger in here? What happened to all the caution and hiding out?"

I shrugged. "The way I looked at it, you were practically dead anyway. What was he going to do?"

Rafe set the empty mug down and took the bottle of water I offered. "But you weren't dying. Believe me, I know these people. They wouldn't hesitate to kill you, too, even if it was just for being in the same house as me."

I shook my head. "Yeah, I know that. But if you were going to die, my job was over anyway. I was okay with going down fighting."

He looked up me, his expression unreadable. And then he wrinkled his nose and made a face. "Gah! There's something wrong with this water. It tastes like shit."

I pushed it back toward him. "Nothing's wrong with it. It has your other meds in it. Drink up."

He curled his lip again, but he turned the bottle up and swallowed some more. "No offense, but you're kind of a bitch, you know?"

"Aw, Rafe, you say the sweetest things. Come on, you're just figuring this out now?"

He rolled his eyes, but I almost thought I might have seen a smile.

"So where's this doctor now?"

"His name is Dr. Eli. He said he'd be back to check on you in a few days. He's old, and he was here until after midnight, so he probably needs to catch up on his sleep."

"Yeah." Rafe finished the water and flipped me the bottle. I caught it easily. "So you want to tell me how you held me down before? I was blocking you. I block all the time, it's just force of habit."

"Oh, didn't I mention that the blocks don't work on me?" I shot him another smile, this one full of triumph.

Rafe coughed, but it wasn't a fit this time, just a nice, dry one. "No, you didn't. Why is that?"

"I worked a way around them when I was hanging out with Zoe. She doesn't know, and neither does Cathryn. I don't plan to use my abilities against anyone from Carruthers, so it's okay. I promise. But it's why I was able to get into the camp in Georgia and fight Mallory's people. Or at least part of why."

"Huh." Rafe sank down farther in the blankets. His eyes were heavy again.

"Are you feeling any better?" I leaned against the doorway, watching him.

His face darkened. "I'm okay. I don't want to be okay. You should have left me in that camp, Nell. And if you couldn't do that, once you got me here and realized how broken I am, you should have let the pneumonia take me. Did you ever think maybe you keep cheating death for me, and one of these days, it's going to catch up?"

He made me so angry sometimes, this ungrateful man

who I'd run myself ragged for the last four days. I took a deep steady breath, but not before a picture frame across the room on the dresser flew up and landed with a crash against the wall.

Rafe's eyes opened wide, and he stared at me.

"No, I don't think I'm cheating death for you. I think I keep saving your sorry ass, and one of these days, you might be glad I did. Clearly today is *not* that day. So you go ahead and lay in here and feel sorry yourself. Me? I'm happy to be alive, and I'm happy you're alive, too. I don't know where the shovels are here, and dragging your carcass out to bury you would be a bitch."

I swung around and left the room, wishing I could slam the door but knowing I needed to leave it open to hear Rafe in case he needed me. I plopped myself on the sofa and sat there, my arms crossed, seething. Zoe had prepared me for his mental state, or she had at least tried to. I'd thought I could deal with it. But God almighty, he annoyed the crap out of me with his 'just-let-me-die' whining.

I laid my head against the back of the sofa, closed my eyes and tried to calm down. I couldn't afford to lose control. Just now it had been a picture frame breaking, but it could all too easily escalate to people and bigger objects. Like cars and trees and knives. And earthquakes.

I began to doze, and I might have actually fallen asleep if a squirrel hadn't jumped onto the porch swing outside, knocking it against the wall. I startled, saw the little guy through the window and lay my head down again. But an odd sensation kept me from drifting off. It was as though someone were scratching at a locked door, if that door were inside my head. I opened my eyes, alert.

I cast my mind as far as I could, just as I had earlier, as I did as a matter of course several times a day. Nothing. Well, nothing but Rafe. And then, as the probing became more insistent, I knew what he was doing, the jackass.

I stood and walked into the bedroom. He lay motionless, his eyes closed, but I knew he wasn't asleep; his mouth was tight and his jaw clenched. When he heard my footsteps, he slitted open his eyes, watching as I drew closer.

I kept my steps even until I reached the bed. I leaned over him to pick up the pillow next to his, and I held it just over his face, staring down at him as I moved it ever closer, inch by inch, until it covered his mouth and nose.

And then I put my mouth up to his ear.

"Nice try, you son of a bitch."

I tossed the pillow back onto the bed and stood back, my arms crossed on my chest. Rafe glared at me.

"So you can block me, but I can't keep you out? In what fucked up way is that fair?"

I snorted. "Who ever said anything about fair? God, Rafe, everything you've been through the last year, and you think there's something out there keeping things even? I knew better than that when I was seven years old. And in what fucked up way is it fair to use me to do your dirty work? Seriously? Did you even stop and think how I would have felt after I'd smothered you? The guilt? Don't I have enough of that to live with?"

"A person who doesn't want to live anymore should be allowed to make that choice." He shot back the words at me, full of venom.

"No, because we call people like that crazy!" I tapped my forehead. "Mental issues. And I should know.

Committed to a psych ward at age seventeen, thanks very much. I know crazy. I lived it and breathed it for a long, long time. And you, my friend, are chock full of it."

"You don't know what I've been through." He stared up at the ceiling, his throat working. "You have no idea what it was like."

"Then why don't you tell me?" I tilted my head, challenging him.

His eyes snapped with fire. "You want to hear all about it? Fine." He stopped to cough, the tension in his body make the spasm that much worse. I forced myself not to step forward to help him. When he could speak again, his words were flat and emotionless.

"We were trying to get away. We'd planned to leave as soon as Ian fixed the car, but then he brought back a surprise. Mallory Jones. As soon as I saw her, I knew we had to get out. We ... we had seen her in New Orleans. She had seen us. The minute she spotted us at the camp, we were as good as dead. But we tried to run. They chased us, but even then, I thought we had a chance. Until Mallory struck. I got blown up against the tree, and when I opened my eyes, it was all over. Everything. I was dead at that minute. I just have to wait for my body to catch up."

"Bullshit." My words were harsh, but I kept my tone gentle. "I get it, Rafe. I know loss. Grief is ... powerful. But you can't stop living. Not when so many people still want you to stay alive. Including Jocelyn."

He was sitting up in a moment, pushing himself with his left hand, rage on his face.

"You don't get to say her name. Never. You didn't know her, and you don't get to talk about her like you did.

And don't fucking try to psychoanalyze me. Just leave me alone."

It was enough for now. I backed out of the room, leaving him one parting reminder.

"I'll be back in an hour with your next dose of medicine."

I couldn't hear his reply, but I could guess at it.

CHAPTER
12

RAFE DIDN'T FIGHT ME on the medicine for the rest of the day. He also didn't speak to me. I kept up a steady chatter as I handed him the mug and water, helped him to the bathroom and got him settled back in the bed. And chatter didn't come easy to me. Talking without getting a response was downright painful. But he was stubborn, and he never said a word, no matter what I asked or what outrageous thing I said.

Just before ten, I took in his final dose for the day. "This is it. If you keep improving tomorrow, I'll only make you take the medicine in the morning and the evening."

Nothing.

He finished his tea and water, and I flipped back the covers and let him lean on me as we made yet another trip to the bathroom.

"You're actually much better." I was surprised, remembering Doc saying Rafe would be weak for days at least. "I think you can almost make this yourself."

Silence.

I settled him back under the blankets and turned off the

light. "Good night, Rafe. If you need anything, I'll be right out here. Of course, since you're not talking to me, I guess you'll probably just lie there and suffer."

I made my way to the sofa and kicked off my shoes. It was the first night since we'd been up here that I hadn't collapsed into sleep, so I took a few minutes to strip off my jeans and reach beneath my shirt to unhook my bra and thread it out through a sleeve of my t-shirt. Sleeping in relative comfort felt like a luxury.

I snuggled down beneath the quilt and closed my eyes. With my last bit of awareness, I listened for anything amiss, both in the cabin and in a wide circle around the mountain. Everything was quiet, and I slipped into sleep.

Rafe kept up the silent treatment the next morning. I decided two could play at that game, and I brought him his medicine without a word. After he drank it all, he rolled over so his back was toward me.

I stomped off, and a few minutes later, I heard the bed creak. Out of the corner of my eye, I saw him shuffling slowly toward the bathroom, clutching the sheet. I remembered I hadn't given him back his clean clothes and grinned to myself. If he wanted them, he'd damn well have to ask.

Right after I took him a bowl of soup—my cooking prowess now extended to opening a can into a pot, adding water and heating up the whole thing—there was a knock at the cabin door. I went on high alert, but a quick scan told me it was Doc. That same peaceful presence calmed my nerves.

"Hey there, Miss Nell." He greeted me with a warm smile. "You look a little bit more rested than the last time I saw you. How's our patient?"

I grimaced without meaning to, and Dr. Eli hooted with

laughter. "That good, huh? A regular prodigy, I guess. Well, let's take a look."

I trailed him into the bedroom. Rafe was sitting up. He stared at our visitor with veiled hostility.

"Don't you look peppy." Doc stuck out his hand. "Dr. Eli Alva. Good to meet you, young man."

For a minute, I was afraid Rafe was going to be rude to the man responsible for saving his life. If he did that, I knew I wouldn't be able to keep my mouth shut. But he only hesitated for a beat before he shook the older man's hand.

"You gave Nell and me quite a scare. I've been dealing with sick people for a long time, and you, my boy, were in bad shape. Mind if I take a look at you?"

Rafe took a deep breath and nodded. I backed out of the room.

"I'll just give you some privacy." I stood on the other side of the door in the hallway, just out of sight of the bed.

Everything was quiet as Doc went about his exam. Finally he sighed deeply, and I heard the chair next to the bed squeak.

"How are you feeling?"

I wondered if Rafe would answer him, but after a cough, he spoke. "Better. The cough isn't as bad. And I think I'm stronger than yesterday. I can make it to the bathroom without help."

"Well, that's really something. Most people who are as sick as you were need a week or so to get back on their feet. You're moving along at quite a clip."

The sheets rustled. "I've always been a fast healer. Guess I'm just lucky." I heard the irony in those words, but if Doc did, he ignored it.

"That you are. I'd say some of that luck is in having Nell as your champion. That girl worked hard, and she fought to keep you on this earth. I hope you're not giving her any trouble."

Silence again, and then Rafe blew out a breath. "I guess I am."

"Hmph. And why would that be? I'd think you'd be grateful."

"Maybe she worked too hard. Maybe she should have just let me go."

"What kind of crazy talk is that?" There was a thump as Doc's feet hit the floor. "Life is a precious gift, boy. You don't throw it away with both hands. You hold on tight, and when someone helps you keep it, you thank her. You appreciate it. You got it?"

Rafe coughed again before he replied. "Yeah."

"Good." I saw Doc's shadow stretch as he stood up. "You keep that in mind ... Raphael."

Footsteps drew near the door, but before I could duck away and hide my eavesdropping self, Rafe voice floated out to me, anger in the words.

"What did you just call me?"

Doc paused. "Raphael."

"That's not my name. Why did you think it was? Who do you know?"

"Calm down, boy. I don't know what you're talking about. Raphael is the angel of healing, you know. It was just a play on your name, being as you seem to have a knack for getting better fast."

"Oh." Rafe sounded a little more subdued. "Sorry. Someone I know—she calls me that. I thought maybe—

sorry. I guess I'm just paranoid."

I darted out into the kitchen and tried to look busy as Doc came out. He caught my eye and shook his head, grinning.

"Don't try to fool an old fool, my dear. I knew you were out there the whole time."

I gave up my pretense. "I'm sorry he was rude, Doc. He's just ..." I shrugged. "He's been through a lot. He lost someone very close to him, and I brought him up here to recover, I guess. Get past it. Maybe it was a bad idea."

"Honey, you can't make people choose to go on anymore than you can make them choose to be happy. You did your best by Rafe, and pretty soon, he'll see that. He seems like a smart boy."

"Thanks. I hope so." I stared out the window, not really seeing the tree beyond the screen.

"Trust me. But for now, I'd say you don't have to force the meds on him anymore. Keep pushing fluids, make him rest when you can, and try to be patient. He'll come around. But he's a healer, that boy. Not only his body, but his mind and soul, too."

I nodded. "Okay. Thank you."

Doc patted my shoulder and opened the front door. "You know where I am if you need me." He called the words back over his shoulder and thumped down the porch steps. I heard him whistling as he continued down the path, away from the cabin.

I stayed out of Rafe's way for the rest of the afternoon. He walked to the bathroom a few times, and each time he shut the door, I left a new bottle of water on his bedside table and took away the empty one.

When darkness fell, I turned off the lamps, leaving only the hallway light burning so that Rafe could see his way around. I pulled the quilt up to my chin and closed my eyes, trying to shut off my brain.

A click sounded in the bedroom, and that room went dark, too. I listened to my heartbeat and thought about how many nights I'd laid in the dark, alone, wishing for someone to talk to, or some way to make sense of the terrible things I'd done. And now here I was, with a perfectly good human being not twenty feet from me, and yet I'd managed to make him hate me, too. It was a gift, apparently. One I wished I could return.

"Nell?" As if I'd summoned it, Rafe's voice floated out to me.

I swallowed and took a breath, intent on keeping my reply casual. "Yes?"

The dark held our silence for a beat, and then he spoke again. "Thank you for not letting me die. Twice."

I closed my eyes again and smiled. "You're welcome. Twice."

"Good night. See you in the morning."

"I'll be here. Good night."

And the night no longer felt so lonely.

CHAPTER
13

THE GROUND WAS TREMBLING, and I couldn't hold on. But that was all right, because someone had to stop her, and right now, that someone was me. I had to keep her from killing Rafe, from tearing down Harper Creek and destroying the people who cared for me.

"Nell!"

I sat up, awake with a racing heart and panic sluicing through my veins. The whole house was shaking. And Rafe was yelling for me.

He stood in the bedroom, holding onto the frame with both hands. As soon as the sleep cobwebs cleared a little, I realized that this earthquake was coming from me.

I closed my eyes and concentrated on calm. I pushed against the ground, trying to keep it stable.

The cabin settled with one final groan, and then it was still.

Rafe came out into the living room, frowning at me. "What the hell was that?"

I shrugged. "A nightmare. Sorry. I didn't mean to ..." I

waved my hand in the air. "Shake everything up."

He rubbed his jaw. "Not exactly how I wanted to wake up."

We'd been at the cabin for two full weeks now. Rafe was recovered from his bout of pneumonia, aside from a little lingering fatigue. We'd fallen into a routine of careful cordiality: we spoke, but only about the necessities of life and survival, like what we were eating for dinner or who was using the shower first in the morning.

Once I felt sure that Rafe was well enough to be on his own for a few hours, I had chanced a trip to the closest town to stock up on food and some extra clothes for both of us. While my aunts and cousins had left a variety of castoffs in the drawers, they were almost all bigger than me. All I wanted was a pair of jeans that actually fit me.

I hit a few different stores so that I didn't raise suspicion at any one place. No one seemed too interested in me or in who I was, which I took as a good sign. I returned to the mountain with enough supplies to keep us going for a while, since I still wasn't sure how long we would have to stay here. I also brought five burner cell phones I'd bought at five different locations, driving thirty minutes farther just to find more stores that sold them.

Since we now had food in the cupboards, Rafe and I had longer discussions on our meals. Cooking was completely beyond me, and the idea of learning to do it bored me silly. Rafe was able to make a few simple dishes, like grilled cheese sandwiches or scrambled eggs.

"I make killer chocolate chip cookies, too," he told me as we sat the table one evening, finishing the pasta and sauce I'd heated up for dinner.

"I'll have to remember to get chocolate chips next time I go for supplies." I smiled at the thought, and then I saw Rafe's face. It was drawn again, his eyes bleak and his forehead wrinkled.

In my own mind, I'd begun calling that the Joss face. It was how he looked any time we even skirted near the topic of his former undercover partner. Apparently there was some memory connected with Jocelyn and chocolate chip cookies, which was a shame since they were my absolute favorite dessert.

Now, still sitting on the sofa and breathing deep, I tried to change the subject. Rafe was staring at me like I'd grown another head.

"Do you want me to get breakfast together?" I stood up, hoping he couldn't see my shaking legs.

"I'll make eggs." Rafe headed for the kitchen, pausing for a minute in front of me. "What was it about?"

I frowned at him until it dawned on me what he meant. "Oh, the nightmare? Typical stuff. Being back in the camp."

He stopped, his hand on the refrigerator. "Did you cause the earthquake that day?"

I pushed hair back off my face and drew my knees up to my chest. "Yes. I needed a distraction to get you out of there."

"So you split the ground open?"

I lifted a shoulder. "I might have gotten a little carried away."

"I'd say so." He pulled out the egg carton, broke three into a bowl and whipped at them with a fork.

Frowning, I laced my fingers together. "It worked. We got away, didn't we?"

Rafe cut a pat of butter and rubbed it on the pan. "Yeah."
I had noticed that since his conversation with Doc, he didn't
insist that saving his life had been a mistake. It was a nice
change of pace.

"But ... ?" There was an edge to my voice.

"I don't know." He dumped the eggs into the pan, and
the sizzle made my stomach rumble. "That kind of thing ...
we start fighting violence with violence, and when does it
stop? How long before Carruthers starts looking for its own
Mallory Jones?" He dug a spatula out of the drawer and cut
his eyes toward me. "Unless they think they already have
one."

I jumped to my feet and stalked into the kitchen, my
head spinning. "Did you just compare me to that murdering
bitch? How can you say that? Is that what you really think of
me?"

Rafe flipped the eggs. He didn't meet my eyes. "Did you
hurt people when you were there to get me?"

A vision of the two men lying beneath the trees flashed
across my memory. I laid my hands flat on the countertop,
letting the cool of the formica calm me.

"I didn't try to. But I can't say for sure. I know I had to
knock two guys out of my way, because they were coming
at me. I didn't kill them, though."

"Not on purpose. But the trees falling, and the fire, and
the earthquake ... there had to be collateral damage." He slid
the fluffy yellow eggs onto two white plates. "So how does
that make us better than them?"

Hurt flooded my heart, and with it, the need to strike
back. "It makes us better because we're just trying to save
people from what those bastards started. I only went into that

143

camp to get you out before they killed you. They were going to execute you that morning, Rafe, not because of anything you did, but because you pose a threat to them. I knocked a few people down because if I hadn't, they would have thrown me into that hole with you. And right now we'd both be in the ground, probably in a joint grave alongside your precious Jocelyn."

His eyes flared. "I told you not to say her name. *Ever*."

He slammed down the pan and strode into the bedroom, slamming the door behind him. I let out a breath and laid my cheek between my hands on the counter, focusing on just breathing, not thinking. *In and out. Just this moment. Nothing more.*

Because I wanted to run after him and scream. I wanted to shake this whole cabin to pieces around his miserable, ungrateful head. God, for just one minute I wanted the athame back in my hands and the chance to make blood flow.

But no. That wasn't me. "I'm not that girl anymore." I spoke the words aloud, and more than anything, I wished for Zoe. I thought of the disposable cell phones hidden in various spots around the cabin, and the temptation to dig one out and call her was huge. Only the idea that any communication with me might be putting her in danger stopped me. I had used one of the phones already to text in with the question mark. There had been no response, which meant it wasn't safe for us yet.

Not that there had been any signs that we had been followed or found. Unless someone was superior at blocking me, which I doubted, there weren't any people with abilities for miles around, other than Rafe and me. But I couldn't shake the feeling that we weren't quite out of danger yet.

I glanced down at the two plates of eggs Rafe had left on the counter. My appetite was gone, but we couldn't afford to waste food. I covered them up and put them into the fridge.

Rafe stayed in the bedroom the rest of the day. As the sun began to set, I went out to sit on the porch, hoping the soft breeze might settle the nerves jumping around my stomach. Caring about what other people thought was a pain in the ass. I hadn't bothered with the opinions of family or anyone else since I was seven years old. I'd made that decision to save my sanity after my mother was locked up.

But now here I was, hurt because Rafe thought I was a cold-blooded killer. Worrying about what Cathryn and Zoe would think of the decisions I was making up here. It was tiresome. The old Nell would tell them all to fuck off, while she did whatever she wanted.

But the new-and-maybe-improved Nell was seriously thinking about knocking on the bedroom door and apologizing to the boy who had questioned my methods when I was saving his life.

Before I could do it, though, I heard footsteps as Rafe walked into the kitchen. I closed my eyes, listening to the cabinet door open, the sound of a plate being set on the counter, a drawer sliding out ... he was making a sandwich. I wanted to tell him to eat the eggs he'd made that morning, but it didn't seem a good lead-off for a reconciliation.

I expected him to take his food and go back into the bedroom, but instead, the screen door creaked open as he leaned out.

"Are you hungry? Because I made a couple of sandwiches. If you want one."

I stared out into the twilight. "I could eat."

"Cool." The door slammed shut, and then a few minutes later, he came out with the plates. He handed me one and sat down on the step, balancing the food on his knees.

We ate in silence, but it wasn't the thick, painful quiet from earlier.

"It's beautiful up here." Rafe finished his sandwich and set the plate on the porch floor. "I forget, sometimes, with all the life and death shit. It's summer now, isn't it?"

We hadn't talked about how long Rafe had been a prisoner at the camp. It fell into the category of things that were just a little too tender still. And up here in the mountains, there weren't computers or phones to tell him the day of the year.

"Yes. It's the end of June now." I paused for a minute and took the last bite of my sandwich. After swallowing, I added, "You were down in that hole for nearly three months."

"Three months." He hunched over, rubbed one hand over his face. "God. She's been gone for that long."

I didn't respond. This was the first time Rafe had mentioned Jocelyn and her death of his own volition. I didn't want to set him off again.

"Do we have scissors?"

I frowned at the random change of subject. "Yeah, in the kitchen drawer. Why?"

"My hair is driving me crazy. I want to cut it."

I stood up. "Here, give me your plate. I'll take it in and get the scissors. Better to do it out here on the porch."

Dropping the plates in the sink to wash later, I dug around in the drawer until I found the scissors. I grabbed a towel out of the bathroom cupboard and dragged a kitchen chair onto the porch.

"Sit down." I pointed to the chair.

Rafe turned around from the step. "What are you doing?"

"I'm going to cut your hair for you."

His brows knitted, he stood up slowly. "Are you sure that's a good idea? Have you ever cut hair?"

I shook my head. "Nope. But I've also never rescued someone from being killed, or made an onion poultice, or lived alone with guy in a remote cabin. Apparently this is my year of doing new things."

He eyed me. "Yeah. Well, I'm the one who has to go around with bad hair if you butcher it."

"Look, buddy." I put my hands on my hips and cocked my head. "It's not like you're standing outside a barber shop. Your options are me or you. And I think I can do it better than you can. Besides, even if I do screw it up, I'm the only one who's around to see you. So if I don't do a good job and I have to look at you for weeks until it grows back, I'll only have myself to blame. Right?"

Rafe studied me again for a minute. "Your logic is a little fucked up, you know that? But okay. Why not? I've trusted you with my life. What's a little hair between friends?"

Friends. I froze as he settled down into the chair. This morning he had been comparing me to a stone-cold killer, and tonight we were friends. And he was questioning *my* logic?

He sat down in front of me, and I draped the towel around him. I tried to remember any hair cut I'd ever had, but it had been so long ... in the hospital, no one had been trotting me off for weekly salon visits.

I threaded my fingers through the length. His hair was silky and soft, nearly as dark as my own. It sifted through my fingers, oddly sensual. Just as when I touched his skin, I felt that disconcerting pulse of power and want.

"I think it needs to be wet first. Your hair, I mean." I rolled my eyes at myself. Double entendre much? And speaking of wet ... I swallowed hard and pulled my hands away from him.

"Let me get some water." I darted into the house, found a pitcher and filled it with warm water. Rafe hadn't moved when I came back.

"Why don't you lean over the rail, and I'll just pour it over your head?"

He complied, and I laid one hand on the back of his neck, sucking in my breath as always when the connection of skin-on-skin hit me. I drizzled the water over his head, adding more until it was dripping.

"Okay." My voice was husky, and I cleared my throat. "You can sit back down."

I picked up the scissors again and began snipping at the back first, trimming it little by little. Absorbed in making it even, I startled a little when Rafe spoke.

"You feel that, too, don't you? When you touch me ... that shock."

I paused for a beat. "Yes. I did from the first time, in the car that day, when I was projecting. I didn't know you did."

"Yeah."

I got the back to a decent length and moved to the first side. "Do you think it has to do with our King connection?

Power calling unto power or something?"

"I guess it might. I don't know, though. I've never felt it before, and I've touched people from other First Families." I hesitated, considering. "Yes, I have, too. You can't live in King and not at least shake hands with other First Families. When I was little, there used to be parties. I remember playing with other kids who had abilities. It was wild."

Rafe shifted, careful not to disturb my work. "I only came to town for visits, but Gram and Gramps have talked about the parties. Why did they stop?"

"I don't know that they did." I trimmed up around his ear, concentrating on not cutting off anything vital. "But after my mother was gone, I didn't go anymore." I stood back, inspected his head. "Okay, turn this way now, please."

"How's it looking?" He sounded just a little nervous.

"So far, so good. Now keep still." The back of my hand grazed his cheek, and Rafe closed his eyes. I stood without moving, letting the sensation wash over me again.

"What do you think it means? This feeling?" His lips barely moved.

"Not sure. All I know is that it seems to boost my power. Projecting that first day was incredible. No swirling vortex, no walking through water ... it was just like being up here, even though my body stayed in the car."

"Swirling vortex?" He opened his eyes and swiveled them back to look at me without turning his head.

"When I projected before, either using blood or Cathryn and Zoe's help, getting there was dicey. I was sucked into something that made me dizzy, maybe a little nauseated. And when I got where I was going, it felt ... thick. Like when you're walking through water. Or underwater."

"Huh."

I finished the other side. It was looking pretty good for my first haircut, if I did say so myself, but I still had to tackle the front.

"Close your eyes. I need to do the front, and I don't want to have to worry about gouging out an eyeball."

"Yeah, I'd appreciate it if you didn't." Rafe's words almost slurred; his face was calm, probably more so than I had seen it, ever.

"You okay?" I combed the top and held a section between two of my fingers.

"Yep. Just ... I feel like I could just fall asleep right here. This is very relaxing."

I moved to stand in front of him, and in order to reach the top of his head, I had to almost straddle his lap, with one leg on either side of his. His face was between my arms, with my chest close to his mouth. If he were to open his eyes, he'd be looking right down my shirt.

Heat built in my center and radiated outward. I had to focus on keeping my hands from shaking, and my breath came in short puffs. The closer I stood to Rafe, the more I could feel the waves of energy and power. It was like a drug, something I wanted more of, right now.

I let my eyes wander down to his face, the shadows of his eyes and the rough hair on his jaw and cheeks. My fingers itched to touch it, to run over the planes and across to his lips, to trace them and slip just one inside.

"Nell?"

I jumped as Rafe's eyes opened and met mine. There was a question there, and I wasn't quite certain what he was asking me. My fingers had stilled in his hair, and I was hyperaware of each place our bodies touched: the sides of my knees against his legs, my arms hovering over the side of his head and my fingers on his scalp.

"Sorry." I whispered it, even though I hadn't meant to. "I was thinking of something. I got distracted."

"It's okay." He was whispering, too, his eyes holding mine.

I didn't move for a moment, and then I tore my gaze from his face. "I'm almost done." I spoke in a nearly-normal voice. "And I promise, it doesn't look bad. I mean, I'm no Vidal Sassoon, but maybe you'll be more comfortable."

I made a few last cuts, stood back and regarded him. My heart was beginning to slow to its normal rate, and I tried to convince myself that whatever I'd felt, standing so close to Rafe, had been a fluke.

"Okay." I brushed off his shoulders and pulled away the towel. "Go look in the mirror and check it out. Oh, and remember, I offer no promises on the service. No money back guarantees."

"Lucky I didn't pay any money to get back." He stood up and shot me a grin. It was the first real smile of his that I'd seen, and it dazzled me right down to my toes.

If Rafe noticed I was suddenly a statue, he didn't remark on it. He strode inside, the screen door smacking on the frame behind him. I closed my eyes, swaying.

God, what *was* that? What in the world was wrong with me? This was a job, an assignment. And even if it weren't, I wasn't some boy-crazy chick, ready to fall in love the first time a guy flashed a smile at me. I had never been that girl. I dated in high school, but I did the choosing, based on what

I wanted and needed, never on what hormones might dictate. Men were there to be used; they were not to be let in where they might take away power and freedom.

"It looks good." Rafe came back out, still smiling. "You may have found your calling. Once this is all over, you can get a job at a hair salon."

I rolled my eyes. "Sure. And the first time a customer pisses me off, I'll set her on fire. Nah, I think I need something with less interpersonal contact. I'm not a people person. I don't play well with others."

Rafe stuck his hands in the pockets of his jeans and looked down on me. His grin had faded now, and his eyes were serious.

"Maybe you need to rethink your view of yourself, Nell. I don't know who told you all those things, but I don't see it. When I look at you, I see a brave, strong and stubborn woman. Someone with compassion and selflessness."

I closed my eyes. "I'm still the same person who tried to kill another human being. Twice. Not out of panic or self-defense, but because I wanted more power. Like you said this morning, maybe I'm not that different from Mallory."

Rafe sighed and ran a hand through his hair. "Shit, Nell. I didn't mean that. Don't listen to me. I was just—your power. It's ... amazing. Sometimes it scares me a little. That's what I was dealing with this morning. I was wrong to say it." He stuck out his hand, an awkward peace offering that hung between us for a fractured second before I glanced up and met his eyes.

"Friends?"

As though of its own accord, my small white hand rose to meet his large tanned one. The minute our skin touched, I fought to keep from throwing my head back and moaning. I swallowed it down and forced a smile.

"Friends."

CHAPTER 14

"HOW WILL WE KNOW when it's safe to go back to Florida? Do you have any idea how much longer we'll be here?"

I was standing at the sink, washing dishes, when Rafe spoke. It had been a week since his haircut, which I deemed a success since he wasn't complaining about it. We had come to a compromise about household chores: Rafe handled the cooking, and I did the dishes. We'd discovered after a few burnt meals that it was better for everyone this way.

"I don't know for sure. I have a way that I check in every once in a while to see if it's safe or not, if they want us to come back So far, nothing."

"How do you check in?" He frowned.

I scrubbed a plate with the wet cloth. "I text a question mark to the number she gave me and wait five minutes. When things calm down, she'll respond, but for now, it's been radio silence."

"What do you mean, when things calm down?" Rafe leaned his back against the counter and folded his arms over his chest. And what a chest it was, broad and firm. The muscles in his upper arms were defined and hard, and I just wanted to run a finger tip over them ...

Gah! I had to get over this. For the past week, I'd been having to work hard to hide what I had to assume was some weird, magic-related infatuation. For over a month, I'd taken care of this guy without a second thought, lived alongside him, and yet now, every time I looked his way, I wanted to throw myself against his body and just see what happened next.

"Umm ..." My mind had taken a detour, and I tried to remember what Rafe had asked. "Oh. Well, I don't know details, but from what Cathryn said, rescuing you was just one part of their plan. Once they were sure that you were safe, I think they were going to try to take down that group, or at least find out how involved their plan was. All Cathryn said to me was that they knew about there were weapons heading to the camp in Georgia. What I overheard when I was there—well, projecting there—told us it was bigger than just that."

"Yeah." Rafe's jaw tightened. "A lot bigger. There's so much I could tell Cathryn now. I didn't think of it before. The Hive—that's what they call themselves. I heard them when I was in the hole. The Hive. They talked about the queen now and then, and the drones ... those are the ones who don't have any powers. But they want to start all this chaos, fires in every city, weapons distributed to the drones ... Carruthers needs to know. All I could see was the pain I was in. If more people die because I was in the middle of a pity party—"

"Rafe, don't." I dried my hands and turned to mirror his position against the opposite counter. "We're doing what

Carruthers instructed us. Cathryn said they could work more efficiently the longer Mallory's group was in the dark about our connection. About the existence of Carruthers, even. We're keeping other agents safe. We need to sit tight and wait."

Rafe dropped his head back, staring up at the ceiling. "Waiting has never been my strong suit. And I keep thinking of my grandparents. I hate that they don't know if I'm dead or alive."

I chewed on the side of my lip. "I might have a solution to that." I opened a kitchen drawer, pulling it all the way out of its slot, and reached back into the empty space.

"Disposable cell phone." I held it out to him, and he took it. "I bought a bunch of them right after we got here. They're hidden all over the cabin, just in case ... well, at first, I was afraid if I told you about them, you might do something crazy."

Rafe quirked an eyebrow. "Like what? Call a cab?"

"I don't know, maybe. Anyway, here's one. I'll show you where the others are. The only thing I ask is if you use one, destroy it, and then tell me so I know how many we'll have to replace."

He turned it over in his hand. "Thanks. I don't know what I'd do with it, but it's good to know you trust me."

I grinned. "Yeah, nothing says 'I trust you' like giving someone a burner phone."

He laughed, and again, I had to hold myself back. *Get it together, Nell.*

"Anyway ..." I folded the damp dish towel in half and hung it over the handle of the oven. "Now you know all my secrets."

"Not quite." The side of his mouth lifted in a half-smile.

My heart fluttered. I know, but it did. Where in the hell was this coming from? My heart didn't *flutter*. None of my body parts did, ever. Maybe I was coming down with something, like an aneurism.

"What do you mean?"

"We haven't figured out the deal with our powers. Why we have that, um ... spark."

"Maybe some things are meant to remain a mystery." I pushed off the counter and made to leave the kitchen, but Rafe shot out an arm to block the doorway.

"I think we should experiment. I mean, we've got nothing but time here. I'm getting bored, and when I get bored, I get restless. And then I start thinking of things I really don't want to remember."

"Experiment?" My mouth went dry. "What do you mean?"

"You know your projection gets a boost when we're touching. I want to know if your other powers do, too. And what about mine?"

I glanced up at him. His eyes were teasing.

"What about yours? Who do you think you're going to experiment on?"

He shrugged, still smiling. "We'll see. Come on out onto the porch. Let's play."

Maybe I was crazy, maybe I was having a late-onset case of teenage-type puppy love, but at that moment, if Rafe had said we were going to the moon, I would have followed.

He sat down on the porch swing and pointed to the cushion next to him. "Sit here."

I perched on the edge, bracing my feet on the floor, with

my hands on my knees. Rafe turned sideways, facing me.

"Okay, let's start with something simple. Can you move that chair across the porch?"

I gave him my are-you-kidding-me look. "Seriously? I could do that when I was three." Without me even breaking our gaze, the chair slid from one side of the porch to the other.

"Okay. Now ..." He held out his hands, palm up. I stared down at them for the space of several breaths. This was just an experiment, but somehow it felt bigger. Like I was about to pass a point of no return.

I lifted my hands and laid them just above his, our palms and fingers not quite touching. Rafe raised his a fraction of an inch, and the push of power slammed through me. This time, I couldn't help it; I arched my neck and groaned. It was as though I'd completed a connection, and everything felt possible.

It was difficult to think clearly, but I did look at Rafe. His eyes were closed and his jaw clenched as though he were in pain.

"Are you okay?" I breathed, not breaking the connection.

"Yes." He ground out the word through gritted teeth. I wondered if he were in pain.

"What now?" I had ideas, lots and lots of ideas, but this was his show.

"Move the chair again."

Before the words were out of his mouth, the chair flew off the porch and high into the air. It executed several neat flips and then shot like a rocket down the mountain and disappeared.

I watched it, my mouth slightly ajar. I hadn't done that ... had I? And yet, how else did it happen?

"My God, someone's going to get the shock of his life when our porch chair lands on his roof. Or in his backyard." I laughed, picturing the chair careening across the sky.

"Or on his car while he's driving." Rafe was grinning down at me, his eyes full of humor and delight, and God almighty, it took my breath completely away, as though I were in that chair, flying in thin air with no thought of landing.

I leaned forward, just slightly, every molecule of my body wanting to be closer to him, touching him from head to toe, with nothing between us.

Rafe cast his eyes upward, thinking. "So touching definitely gives you extra juice."

Oh, buddy, you don't know the half of it.

I nodded.

"My turn, then. Let's see if the power flows in both directions." He folded his fingers so they gripped my wrists, our palms still sealed together. A second sweet shock jarred me, but I was thriving on it now, sucking it in and letting the sensation consume me.

Rafe screwed shut his eyes. I watched him, savoring the chance to look at his face without it being stalker-creepy. His mouth was relaxed, lips just a little parted, and they intrigued me. He had found a razor a few days ago and used it, but since then, some of the scruff had grown back. I wondered if he would notice if I were to lean forward and brush my cheek over his, just to see what it felt like ...

And then I was moving toward him, compelled by a force I couldn't disobey. My lips opened as they crept closer to Rafe's mouth, and after a hesitation that wasn't long enough for a thought, I was kissing him.

Kissing had never been a big deal to me. I'd tried it in high school, the same way I'd tried a lot of other things. As a prelude to sex, it was fine, but it didn't set me on fire. I could do without it.

But what I was doing with Rafe right now ... it went right up there next to breathing. I angled my head to get deeper, and his answering pressure sent a glad thrill down to my core.

When his tongue danced around mine, teasing, I moaned, almost a sob. Our hands were still connected, keeping me from bringing my body too close to his. But that was all right, because at the moment, only our lips and tongues existed. Rafe traced the inside of my mouth with the tip of his tongue, caressing. He sucked at my lower lip and then took my mouth again, moving his lips with intensity. I thrust my tongue forward, touching his and swirling it in a seductive circle.

I don't know how long we sat there, me tilted forward, Rafe meeting me halfway. Just when I thought I might incinerate if he didn't touch me somewhere, anywhere, he pulled away and leaned his forehead to mine.

"I call that a hit."

I sat back, my head still spinning, and I tugged my hands from his grip. Rafe rubbed his palms over his jeans, and that stung. Was he wiping away my touch? This had all been a joke to him?

"You manipulated me." It all made sense now.

"Yeah." Rafe looked all too pleased with himself. "And it worked. Even with your blocks up. So us touching does increase my abilities, too."

"You son of a bitch."

Rafe's face folded into a frown of confusion. "What?"

"You used me. You made me—us—you fucking bastard." I stood up, and the swing banged against the side of the porch. The screen door opened and slammed, and the windows trembled in their frames. I closed my eyes and breathed deep, focusing to rein in the power.

Once I had it tamped down, I turned on my heel and stomped inside, this time slamming the door with my hand. I walked halfway through the cabin before I realized that I didn't have a room to hide in. Sitting down on the sofa in righteous indignation somehow didn't have the same oomph as storming into a room and giving a good wall-rattling door slam.

Rafe had followed me inside. I glared at him, anger and hurt battling inside me for the upper hand. There was so much I wanted to say, but unexpected words came tumbling out of my mouth.

"I want the bedroom. It's my cabin. You're not sick anymore, and I've been sleeping on that damn sofa for over a month. I'm a girl. I need privacy, and God damn it, I need my own room." I stamped my foot. Childish, yes, but I didn't care.

Rafe frowned. "Okay, sure. All you had to do was say it."

"Fine." I wheeled around and went into the bedroom, giving the door a good hard shove behind me. I tore the comforter off the bed and dropped it in the corner, and then stripped the sheets. I scooped them into my arms and went back out, ignoring Rafe, who stood in the same place I'd left him. I hauled the bedding to the washing machine and dumped it in, adding detergent and hitting the button. I stood next to the whirring machine, my hand tapping the lid.

He'd made me so damn angry. One part of me understood. Rafe didn't know how I felt, what I had been thinking. There was a limit to how he could test his own ability while touching me, particularly when his powers had to be used on a human and I was the only available subject. Maybe it would have been better if he had made me recite the Gettysburg Address, but he hadn't.

And he *had* kissed me back. I hadn't imagined that. His tongue touching mine, the pressure of his lips ... had that been just part of the experiment as well?

I stayed outside, sitting on top of the washer, until the sheets finished. I pinned them to the line and went back inside. Rafe was sitting at the kitchen table, but I ignored him as I opened the cupboard beneath the sink and took out the cleaning supplies I'd found there when we moved in. I spent the rest of the afternoon back in the bedroom, dusting furniture, scrubbing down walls and shining windows.

Something smelled delicious as I walked through the house to get the sheets. Rafe stood at the stove with his back to me, but I knew by the way his back stiffened that he heard me.

I had just finished making the bed when Rafe knocked on the door. "Nell, I made dinner. Do you want to eat?"

I closed my eyes. I wanted to say yes. I wanted to go out and sit down with him, pretend this morning had never happened. Would he apologize yet again? Maybe. But I didn't want his apologies or his explanations. I wasn't certain what I wanted from him, but not that.

"I'm fine, thanks." I kept my words clipped.

"Are you sure? It's chicken. I just kind of made it up, but it's not bad. And I can bring you a plate in here if you don't want to eat with me."

"I'm not hungry." That was true.

"Okay." His footsteps retreated from the door, leaving me in silence. It was still light out, but I took off my clothes, climbed under the covers and curled into a ball. I wanted to cry, but nothing came.

I lay there, alone and aching, as shadows crept across the room and night fell.

CHAPTER 15

I WOKE UP IN the early morning, disoriented until I figured out where I was. The day before came flooding back over me, and mortification battled with pain. I tossed and turned for another hour before I got up, pulled on shorts and t-shirt and opened the door.

Rafe was still asleep on the sofa, huddled beneath the quilt and facing the back. I slipped by him and out onto the porch.

The sun was just beginning to paint the sky pink, and the air was still chilled. I huddled on the swing, my arms wrapped around my knees and my heels on the edge of the seat, letting the freshness of the day wash over me.

I didn't know how long I'd been sitting there when the screen door screeched and Rafe stepped out. He walked over to lean against the porch railing, facing me. I tried not to notice the way his jeans slung low over his hips or the gap of skin visible where his t-shirt had ridden up.

"Morning." He tucked the tops of his fingers into the pockets of his jeans.

"Hey." I stared past him into the trees.

"Do you want breakfast? I can make French toast."

I lifted one shoulder. "Not really."

"Nell." He hunched over, staring down at his bare feet. "I'm not sure why you were so mad yesterday. I'm guessing I crossed a line, and if that's what happened. I'm sorry. Again. God, I feel like I'm always apologizing to you."

I flashed a look at him, and he held out his hands, palms toward me.

"Not that I shouldn't. Not that it wasn't called for. I'm not saying that. Just ... I guess I'm a jerk. I thought you knew what I was going to do yesterday. I couldn't think of another way to try it out. In all honesty, I didn't think it was going to work. Your blocks are so strong."

"I didn't have them up. I didn't think I needed to, when it was just you and me working together. I trusted you." My tone made it clear that wasn't going to happen again any time soon.

Rafe closed his eyes and rubbed the back of his neck. "I know. I thought of that after. But at the time, I guess I just got carried away. That feeling when we touch ... there's something almost ..." He stopped and looked down at me, his eyes clouded.

"Almost?" I prompted.

He shook his head. "Nothing. It doesn't matter, that's an excuse. Nell, I get that you think I was out of line, but I don't understand why you got so mad. It didn't mean anything. It was just a kiss."

"Just a kiss." I nodded. "I guess you would see it like that. I read your file, so I know all about your adventures last summer."

Rafe's head snapped back like I'd struck him. "What in the hell is that supposed to mean?"

I spread out my hands. "You're used to using your powers to get what you want. Manipulating women so they'll sleep with you. I'm sure yesterday was like old times with you. And pretty amusing, too, probably, when I fell for it."

"That's not true. First of all, I never use my powers to make women have sex with me. Want to know the truth? I never had to."

I snorted and rolled my eyes.

"Second, what happened yesterday was not about me using you. Or making fun of you. Why would you think that?"

"Because I'm not that kind of girl. I'm not the type of girl who boys want to kiss. I'm a cold, controlling bitch. A killer. A psycho. I'm the one everyone leaves."

"Nell." Rafe had the grace to look miserable. "I'm sorry. I didn't mean to—"

"Don't you dare feel sorry for me." The calm I'd found earlier disappeared, replaced with a good solid mad and a bubbling pool of energy just begging to be unleashed.

"I don't feel sorry for you, I'm sorry for what I did."

That was the final straw, that he would regret the kiss that had been one of the most beautiful moments of my life before he ruined it. I stood up. Rafe must have seen the fire in my eyes, because he backed up toward the porch steps.

"You're sorry. You used your mind to make me kiss you, and I get that it was to check out the power boost. But then *you kissed me back*. You could have made me give you a simple peck on the lips, and we would have laughed it off. But it was so much more. You took that connection, and what it makes us feel, and you made it hurtful and horrible."

The wind began to blow, and trees around the cabin creaked ominously. Rafe glanced around, frowning.

"All I've done is tried to be a better person. I've bitten my tongue, I've held in my powers. And what did it get me?"

The ground began to shake.

"Nothing. It got me absolutely freaking nothing. It got me a kiss like I never imagined, and then I found out the other person in it with me thought it was a big joke." I ended on a growl, and the cabin trembled.

Debris flew through the air. A branch broke off a nearby tree and hit Rafe on the side of his face. Knocked off balance as the porch listed to the right, he reached for the railing but missed and fell down the steps. He landed on the arm that had been hurt at the camp and lay there groaning.

The sight of Rafe on the ground stopped me cold. With painful effort, I pulled everything back within me, stopped the shaking and calmed the wind.

I stumbled down the steps and knelt next to Rafe. He was trying to sit up.

"I'm sorry. I'm so sorry."

"I'm all right." He rolled to his side and pushed up. "Damn. That arm."

"Here, let me help you up." I stretched out my hand. Rafe hesitated for a second before he took it. There was a new bittersweet component to the connection. I wondered if he felt it, too.

An ugly bruise was already visible on the side of his face from where the branch had hit him. Guilt, an all-too familiar emotion, welled up in me. Everything I touched, I ruined. The redemption I thought could be mine was gone.

We were both quiet as I sat him down in the kitchen, checked his arm and carefully touched his cheek.

"I don't think anything's broken." I tied ice into a towel and held it to his face. "The arm ... do you want me to go get Doc?"

"No." Rafe shook his head. "If we can immobilize it, it'll be okay."

"I can make a sling."

I dug for an old sheet and ripped it into a twelve-inch wide strip. Rafe watched me with expressionless eyes as I looped it around his neck and snugged the injured arm to his body.

"Rafe, I'm sorry. I didn't mean to get so carried away. I was hurt. But I should have shut it down earlier."

He sat there, one arm in a sling and the other holding a bag of ice to his face. His eyes met mine and then skittered away. *Damn.*

"If you want me to leave, I will. You're not sick anymore, and you don't need a babysitter. I can go. I'm dangerous, and I need to be away from people. I'll be gone by tomorrow morning."

"Nell, don't. It wasn't all your fault. Yesterday was more than what I said. It's true I started out just trying to see if I could get through your blocks, but then ... when you touched me, it was more. It was like I could feel you all through me. And you're right. I kissed you back. I don't know why, but I know it was wrong. How could I do that with you when Joss—she's only been gone a little while. I felt like I betrayed her, and when I looked at you and saw your eyes shining, part of me wanted to grab your arms and kiss you again, and the other part needed to make it ... less.

Unimportant. A joke."

"But I hurt you."

He shook his head. "You have powers. You're still trying to get them under control. Today was the first time you've lost it, and I know I've been a pain in the ass to live with. When you said that about the bedroom, I felt like such an idiot. I don't know why I didn't think of it sooner."

"So you don't want me to leave?" Relief made me weak.

"Of course not. Besides, you think I'd let you take my car?"

I frowned. "Your car? What do you mean?"

He gave me that half-smile that melted my heart. "The Impala. That's my car. You didn't know it?"

"No. I only took it because it was open. And the keys were in the ignition. Don't you remember?"

"No. That day is kind of a blur."

"There were two cars. One was a rust bucket, and locked up to boot. The other was the Impala, and it was open with the keys in the ignition."

Rafe shook his head. "I bet Ian fixed it and then was planning to take it with him. Bastard."

We sat there, lost in our own thoughts.

"Nell, I really am sorry about yesterday. I shouldn't have done it, and then I shouldn't have pretended it didn't mean anything. I really just want us to be friends."

I forced a smile I wasn't feeling. "And I'm sorry for almost killing you. Again." I rose. "I guess I'm making breakfast today."

"Are you kidding?" Rafe stood up as well. "Even with one arm, I'm a better cook than you. And I've had all the traumatic experiences I need for this morning."

CHAPTER
16

"WHAT HAPPENED TO YOUR mother?"

I glanced up from the book I was reading. A few days before, while I was looking through the bedroom closet for more warm-weather clothes, I'd come across a treasure trove of old paperbacks. Most of them were romances, which was not a genre I usually enjoyed, but I was so hungry for books that I began devouring them. The only drawback was that the love stories fed into my dreams, which were becoming increasingly detailed, lust-filled and always featuring a man with dark hair and smoky eyes.

Now I blinked at Rafe, reluctant to pull myself out of the story where the heroine was just about to be ravished by the pirate with a heart of gold who had kidnapped her.

"My mother? What about her?"

Rafe was sitting at the kitchen table, playing with the video game I had picked up for him on my last foray into town for supplies. It had been on sale, but it still had taken more cash that I probably should have paid. In the end, though, I'd pictured his arm in the sling and the purple bruise on his cheek, and I bought it. Guilt could be pricey.

But the way his face lit up when I presented it to him back at the cabin made the cost worth it. I knew he was getting restless and bored, anxious to know what was going out beyond the protected parameter of our mountain. I dreaded the day when he would insist we needed to leave. I knew it was coming. If a little hand-held machine that let him chase zombies helped put off that day, I was more than willing to pay for it.

He set the game down on the table and turned in his chair to look at me, where I was curled up on the sofa.

"You mentioned her a little while back. When we were talking about the First Family parties in King. You said you stopped going to them after your mother left. I know something happened. I remember Gram saying it had been a mess, and when Tasmyn talked about you, she said you were looking for a replacement mom figure. But I don't know any details."

I snorted. "Tasmyn Vaughan, amateur psychologist. If you're making judgments about me based on what she said, consider the source."

"I thought you had found some peace with her. You helped her fight Marica at the end, right?"

"True, but we're very different people. Tas and I will never be BFFs."

"Yeah, well, I feel the same. Too much history."

I thought about Tasmyn and what I remembered of her time with Rafe. I could picture his face as she had seen him, naked longing in his eyes as he looked at her, and I swallowed a lump of jealousy.

"But I don't want to talk about her. I want to hear about

your mother and what happened. I mean, if you don't mind telling me."

I stuck a strip of paper between the pages of my book and laid it on the coffee table. "What do you want to know, specifically?"

"What do you remember?"

I closed my eyes. "I remember ... before. A little, anyway. My parents were in love, or they seemed to be. I think we were happy. And then things began to change. My father was at home less and less, and when he was there, he and my mother were fighting. My mom had been teaching me about magic, letting me try a few little things. Growing plants, playing with the wind or with water. But then she wasn't around much, either. And she became ... well, looking back, knowing what was going on, she must have been nervous about being found out. But to the seven-year-old me, it just felt like she didn't want to be with me anymore."

Rafe's brow drew together. "What *was* going on?"

"She was having an affair. Sleeping with a married man. Which would have been bad enough, but then I guess he tried to break it off. At any rate, somehow my mother got the idea that if she got rid of his wife, she and her lover could be together. She was going to kill her. She had the plan all set, even started to put it into action, but she was caught. My dad didn't want the embarrassment of a wife in prison, so he pulled strings and she was committed. I never saw her again."

"God, Nell." Rafe rubbed the back of his neck. "I thought I had it rough when my dad died and my mom remarried, but I was a teenager. You were just a baby."

I rested my head on the back of the sofa. "It was a long

time ago."

"Did you live with your father after that?"

I shook my head. "He was around off and on for a while, but he hated King. I think he made some noise about wanting to take me away, but my mother's family put up a fuss, and gradually he just ... disappeared, too. I saw him a few times a year, and he sent money. Made sure I had everything I needed, materially."

"So who took care of you?"

I shrugged. "Aunts, sometimes. Cousins. My dad hired people to be at the house with me. I never wanted for anything." *Except love, attention and acceptance.*

"I'm sorry, Nell. That sucks. I didn't know."

"Yeah." I toyed with the edge of the quilt that lay over the couch. "But you know, I had a lot of time to think over the past few years. I let what happened with my mom make me who I was. I didn't get much out of the therapy they made me do, but I remember something one of the doctors said. She said we all have shit in our lives, and we can't help that. But it's what we do with it that makes the difference."

Rafe nodded. "That sounds like something Zoe might say."

"She's something else, isn't she?" I grinned. "When I first saw her sitting next to my hospital bed, I thought I was hallucinating."

"That's nothing. I met her the first time on a battlefield in New Orleans. I didn't know who she was. She just came up and started talking to me, and I thought she was some random crazy lady. But she's really cool, you know?"

"She is. She was worried about you." I hesitated. This was a delicate topic, but I'd been trying to broach the topic for a while. "Before I left Harper Creek, she told me that your physical injuries might not be as bad as your emotional ones. She tried to prepare me for that."

Rafe's face tightened. "And was she right?"

I smiled, trying to lighten the mood. "Yep. At least until I tossed you around myself and threw tree branches at your face."

He didn't return the smile. "Zoe's going to want to pick apart my brain when I get back. Great. You know, I was going to suggest that we try to head to Florida soon, but now that I think about it ... maybe not."

"She cares about you. She only wanted to help. That's why she told me about ... everything."

"There's nothing anyone can do to help. It happened. I'm not going to get all touchy-feely about it. I just want to move on."

"But if you don't talk about it—"

"You want to talk about it? You want to hear the dirty details? Fine. Get ready." Rafe stood up and began pacing across the living room. "Those people at the camp? The Hive? The ones planning to burn up the world? We lived with them, got to know them. Most of the people there are decent. They don't know what's going on. Nathan and his cohorts are using them. Or they were, until you came into rescue me. I'm willing to bet most of the collateral damage you talked about hit those men and women. Nathan and Ian called them drones.

"Joss ..." Pain infused his face when he said her name. "Joss and I found out what we could about their plans, and we were ready to leave. We knew we were in more danger the longer we stayed. Ian was bringing the parts back to fix the Impala, and then we were planning to leave. But Ian brought back more than supplies. He brought back their own personal killing machine. Mallory Jones." Rafe spit out the words.

"Did they bring her there because of you and Joss? They knew who you were?"

Rafe shook his head. "I don't think so. I'm pretty sure it was just a bad coincidence. But when we saw her ... Joss and I had run into her at the meeting in New Orleans where she killed a client. We were pretty sure she knew we had abilities, but we didn't think she knew who we worked for. And when I saw her that day in the camp, all I could think was that we needed to get out of there, get away. Fuck the car, fuck the mission."

I clamped my lips between my teeth, dreading what was coming next. Rafe's face was taut with pain.

"So we ran, and they followed, and they caught us in the woods. Even then I thought we'd get away. Joss had telekinesis, you know. Not as powerful as you, but she could move things, so she threw a rock at Nathan's head, knocked him out. She wanted me to get away. I think she knew at that point that we weren't going to both escape, and she was trying to give me the best chance.

"She kept telling me to run. Broadcasting it to my mind, you know. But I wouldn't leave her. I was holding her hand, and I looked at Mallory. The next thing I knew, I was blasted against a tree. I woke up, and I was still holding Joss's hand, but it was just ... limp. And her eyes were staring up at the sky. Empty. She was gone."

A drop of moisture hit my hand, and I raised fingers to my cheek, surprised to find tears there. Rafe had stopped pacing and was staring out the window, his back to me.

"That bitch killed her. And they should have killed me. I know what you say, I know what Doc said, but it's the truth. When they threw me in that hole, they should have shoveled dirt in on top of me."

"Rafe, stop." I wiped at my face. "You have people who care for you, who would be devastated if you didn't make it. Your grandparents. Everyone at Carruthers." I paused and took a breath. "Me."

He turned then, hard eyes fastening on mine. "Don't, Nell. Don't make me into a hero or build some romantic fantasy around me. I'm only here because you wouldn't let me die. Once we can leave, I'm no longer your responsibility, and I'll be out of your life."

The words stung, and I swallowed hard. "I thought we were friends. Your words, remember?"

His answering laugh was harsh. "I can fool myself into believing that sometimes. Doesn't make it right. I'm a bad bet, and I always have been. I ruin everything I touch. So don't go gazing at me with that look in your eye. I'm a self-serving bastard. I use and consume. Do yourself a favor and accept that now."

I jumped to my feet. "I don't know what you're talking about. I don't 'gaze' at you with any kind of look." My face burned, because I knew he was right, and it mortified me that he had noticed. "You're right. You are a bastard, but buddy, don't worry about me. I take of myself, first and foremost. I don't need anyone, and I never have. This job can't be over fast enough, and then you'll never have to think of me again."

I sailed past him and into the bedroom, slamming the

door behind me without even touching it. I had to get away from him before I did something I might regret later. Like throw him off the mountain the same way I did that chair the other day.

Once I was out of the living room, though, the anger dissipated, and only the hurt was left. I huddled on the bed, feeling miserable and sorry for myself. I wouldn't let myself cry anymore, not over him. I screwed shut my eyes to stop the tears that threatened.

At some point, I must have drifted to sleep, because when I opened my eyes, the shadows had moved across the room. It was late afternoon. I rolled over and stared up at the ceiling. I was drained, empty. And hungry. And damn it, I'd left my book in the living room, and I wanted to read.

I composed my face into an expression of utter indifference and opened the door. The cabin was empty. I picked up my book and grabbed some crackers from the kitchen, but there was still no sign or sound of Rafe. Curious, and then worried, I checked the bathroom, the porch and even the laundry lean-to, but he wasn't there.

Panic seeped into me as I circled the cabin for a second time. I couldn't help myself; I stood on the edge of the mountain and called his name.

"Rafe!"

I'd yelled loud enough that the birds in the nearby tree took flight, scolding me and twittering as they went. I knew it was stupid; here we were, trying to keep a low profile, and I was yelling his name from the mountain tops. *Smooth move, Nell.*

And then I heard footsteps. I froze, casting my mind out to check for danger, but there was only Rafe, kicking through the underbrush as he climbed back up to the cabin. I felt weak with relief.

"For God's sake, Nell, you want to let the world know where we are? What are you thinking, yelling like that?" He still sounded aggravated.

I could do mad. "I wouldn't have to yell if you stayed inside, like you're supposed to. I came out, and you were gone." I hissed the words at him, trying to keep my voice down.

Rafe emerged from the trees. He stopped in front of me and cocked his head. "Nell, did you really think I'd leave you? Here, by yourself?"

I curled my lip. "Men leave."

"I don't." His voice gentled, so much the opposite of what it had been earlier in the cabin that my head spun.

"You will." Pain shot through me, and I hid it with a mix of contempt and anger. He was tearing me apart, this boy. One minute he was so sweet I wanted to melt into him, and the next he hurt me worse than I ever thought could be possible.

I felt the power banked within me. I wanted to lash out. Make him fly through the trees, set the cabin ablaze and just disappear. Push him away before he could leave. Protect myself. And then he spoke again, his words thoughtful and measured.

"Nell, I can't promise you anything. Our world is so screwed up. We don't know when the next attack is coming. But you can trust me. As long as it's in my control, I'm staying."

He held out a hand, tentatively, in my direction, and my breath caught. We had avoided all unnecessary touch since the day he kissed me. I ran my tongue over my lips, remembering that, and remembering too how he had hurt me earlier. And yet ... my hand reached out, almost of its own accord. Rafe's fingers tightened around mine.

"Did you ever think you might have multiple personalities?" I whispered.

Rafe laughed, husky and low. "That would explain a lot, wouldn't it?" He looked down at our joined hands and took a deep breath. "Nell, I'm really sorry again. About today. I— talking about the camp and remembering, it just made me crazy. I took it out on you. That was wrong."

I drew in a breath. "Rafe, I'm used to being in control. I'm trying to be a better person, but when you treat me like a friend one day and an enemy the next, it's hard. I don't know what you want from me."

"I understand. None of this is your fault." He rubbed his fingers over my hand. "I like you, Nell. I feel comfortable with you—when we're not fighting, that is." The side of his mouth lifted in that bone-melting half-smile.

"But when I think of Joss, I wonder what's wrong with me. I loved her. I never told her, because we had time. We thought we did, anyway. We always said we'd keep it casual between us, nothing serious. She used to tease me any time she thought I was starting to treat her like a girlfriend. But then things changed, and I thought after we got back to Florida, we could take it deeper. We didn't get the chance to do that. I guess part of me thinks if I can get over her this fast, feel ... attraction to someone else, maybe there's something inherently wrong with me. Maybe I'm like my mom. She got over my dad fast enough."

My heart ached for him, but at the same time, a spark

quivered down my spine. *He said he felt an attraction. To me?*

"I don't think there's anything wrong with you. We're in a unique situation. And I know you got mad at me for saying it before, but if Joss was the kind of person I've heard she was, do you really think she'd want you to stop living?"

Rafe shook his head. "No. As a matter of fact, she told me once that some relationships are like snowflakes, and if we try to hold onto them, they'll only melt and disappear. She said you have to appreciate the beauty while you have it."

I smiled. "That's very profound."

"That was Joss. Wild, wicked and crazy one minute, and yet with so much depth ... she was tough. Like you are. But she had a softer side, too."

"I wish I had known her. Will you tell me about her?"

Rafe nodded. With our hands still linked, we wandered over to sit on the porch steps. We stayed there until sunset, and for a span of time, we both knew peace.

CHAPTER
17

"TOUCH ME, NELL."

Rafe leaned over me, his eyes dark with desire as his hands moved over my breasts. I ran my hand down his back, reveling in the muscles, and then circled to the front of his body, where his throbbing length jutted. When I stroked him, he dipped his mouth to capture the rosy tip of my—

"Nell!"

I opened my eyes, blinking in confusion. My heart was beating fast, and need pulsed between my legs. One hand was over my stiff nipple.

Morning sunlight flooded my room, and another knock sounded at the door. "Nell. Are you okay?"

It had been a dream. *Damn.* I needed to stop reading those smutty romance novels. They were giving me ideas. Bad ideas. Dangerous ideas.

"Uh, yeah. Why?" I cleared my throat and pushed myself to sit up in bed.

"You were moaning in your sleep. I thought you might be sick and need me."

Not sick, but definitely need you.

I gritted my teeth and brushed the hair out of my face. "I'm all right. Just a dream. Sorry if I woke you."

"You didn't. Mind if I come in?"

I gave myself a quick once-over. The sheets covered me from the waist down, but my breasts were free under the t-shirt I wore for sleeping, and they were quite clearly sporting pebbled nipples. I tugged the covers higher.

"Yes, come on in."

The door opened. Rafe was wearing a pair of the shorts we'd picked up a few days ago, when I'd agreed to let him come with me on a supply run. His arm was healed, and the bruise on his face had faded, so I felt it was reasonably safe to take him into town.

He came in and sat down on the edge of the bed, eyeing me curiously. "Are you sure you're not sick? Your face is all flushed."

I shook my head. "No. I mean, yes, I'm sure. I'm fine. It's just warm in here."

"You know you can sleep with the door open, like I used to. It gives you more circulation. And I promise you're safe from me."

What if I don't want to be safe from you?

I smiled. "Okay, I'll remember that. Diyd you need something?"

His eyes lingered on my hair, tousled from sleep—and dreams—and then roamed down the rest of my body. My heart thumped in anticipation, and then plummeted as he forced his gaze to my face.

"Not really. I made waffles for breakfast. I ate mine, but if you don't want any, I need to wrap up the extras."

"Sure. That sounds great. I'll be out in a minute."

"Okay." He stood up, hesitating a minute more before he turned to leave. I collapsed back onto my pillows.

There had been a definite shift in our relationship after our last argument. Rafe was consistently kinder, and he didn't talk about wanting to die anymore. He didn't try to kiss me again, but now and then over the last week, he had reached for my hand when we sat on the porch. I loved the connection, but each time he touched me, I wanted more. Hence, the dreams.

I pulled myself together, put on a pair of shorts and joined Rafe at the table. He pushed a waffle-covered plate in front of me.

"Thanks." I buttered the waffle, added syrup and took a bite. "Mmmm." I closed my eyes, savoring it. "Delicious. Thanks, Rafe."

"You're welcome."

"I have to say, if you must be in hiding with someone for an extended period of time, it's smart to choose someone who can cook." I took another bite.

"Speaking of being in hiding ..." Rafe took a deep breath. "I've been thinking it over. We should go back to Florida."

My stomach clenched. I set down the fork and wiped off my mouth. "Why? What makes you say that?" All my insecurities jumped up to give me the answer: he was tired of being stuck in a cabin with only me, worn out over fighting with me all the time, afraid of what I could do. Pick one.

"Ever since we talked about what happened in Georgia, I've been dreaming about it. About what Mallory's group is planning to do. How many people has she killed while we've been up here, hiding? How many more camps have they armed? I could stop them, and I've been sitting here with my thumb up my ass. I need to get back to work. I'm going stir-crazy."

I nodded, my head spinning. I knew Rafe didn't mean it, but his words crushed me. These months up here in the mountains had been the best of my life, the fighting and the fear notwithstanding. I had space, I had freedom, I had peace and I had Rafe, as a friend, if nothing else. If given the choice, I would have happily stayed here forever.

"You don't agree." His voice tightened with frustration. "Nell, you're a fighter. You're a warrior. I've seen it. How can you be satisfied with sitting on the sidelines, hiding, when we could be making a difference?"

I glanced up at him through my lashes, unwilling to let him see my eyes, lest he read my pain there.

"It's different for me, Rafe. You'll go back to friends and family. A mission. A purpose. I'm Nell Massler, the crazy witch who spent years in a mental hospital. And another year in a coma. That stuff isn't exactly conducive to making friends."

He frowned. "No, that's not true. Cathryn and Zoe—you have them."

I sighed. "I was awakened and activated by Carruthers expressly to bring you home. To save you. Once that's done, do you really think they're going to be interested in keeping someone like me on the payroll?"

"Why wouldn't they? With your talents?"

I rolled my eyes. "Rafe, you might have noticed that I'm not stable. My powers are dangerous and not easily controlled. Up here, where my environment is controlled, I've done better, and yet I still managed to hurt you."

"Zoe can work with you. She did with Joss."

"She would. I'm not saying they would kick me out of the company, Rafe. I'm saying when we go back, once I deliver you, I'm going to disappear. I'm going to live some place remote, away from people. Some place peaceful."

His eyes were troubled. "Why? Like you told me, you have a choice. You can choose to be part of life, not to run away from it."

I laughed, though it was more sadness than mirth. "Those kind of rules work for other people, not for me. Trust me, Rafe. It's for the best. This mission, saving you, was my second chance, and I think I've found a measure of redemption. But that doesn't let me off the hook for everything I've done or might do."

Rafe slammed his hand down on the table, and I jumped. His anger had come out of nowhere.

"Dammit, Nell. You're making this an impossible choice."

My eyes widened. "What choice?"

He stood up and shoved in the kitchen chair. "You're setting me up to choose. As long as I stay up here with you, you're not alone. You have a purpose. But if I decide to go back and fight, I'm sentencing you to life alone. That's bullshit."

I swallowed back a sob that almost took me by surprise. "I've always known you'd go back. I don't expect you to stay here with me out of some misguided sense of obligation. I don't want your pity, Rafe." My own ire was rising, sharp and dangerous.

"Fuck that. I want to go back and *live*, Nell, like you've

been pounding into my head for the last two months. You could have left me at the camp to die, or you could have let me go when I was sick. But you hauled me back from the edge over and over, and now you're saying I have to go back by myself? That I have to live, but you don't? *Fuck that.*"

Before I could suck in a breath, he strode over to where I sat, grabbed me by my upper arms and hauled me to my feet. His mouth was on top of mine, open, hot and devouring.

For a heartbeat, I didn't respond. And then my mind caught up to my body, and my arms were around his neck, clutching his hair, matching him in intensity. I angled my head, giving him access to every inch of my mouth.

Rafe's tongue plunged between my lips. It felt like a prelude of what was coming, and I answered by fitting my body closer to his, rubbing the blazing need in my core against the proof of his desire, hard and long within the confines of his shorts. There was too much between us still, too many barriers. I couldn't think or breathe, I could only be. And all I knew was that I wanted him within me.

Still holding my arms, Rafe walked forward until my back met the bedroom door I'd left ajar. Without removing his lips from mine or missing a beat, he kicked it open and kept going forward until we hit the bedroom wall.

He reached behind his neck to disengage my hands. For a disconcerting moment, I thought he was going to push me away and stop us. But instead, he held both of my wrists in one large hand and raised them to the wall, over my head. I was completely at his mercy, unable to move at all.

He trailed his lips, hungry and searing, down the column of my neck. I threw my head back to give him better access. When I opened my eyes, I could see his hand clutching my arms above me, and that display of his strength was intoxicating.

Rafe's mouth reached the neckline of my t-shirt, teased there at the tops of my breasts. He shoved his free hand up beneath the material, growling against my skin as his fingers found my nipple and pinched gently.

"Do you know how crazy these make me? When you come to breakfast without a bra and I can just see a hint of what you have ... I've been losing my mind, imagining doing this to you."

His mouth dropped to one breast, biting the peak through the cloth of my shirt, even as his fingers continued to torture the other one. I gasped and arched to give him more, longing to hear more, to feel more. Liquid heat flooded me, and I knew I was wet and ready for his touch. God, I was almost coming just from him touching my breasts. Now if he didn't move his hands between my legs ...

I wanted to feel him, to wrap my hands around the hardness I could see, but my hands were still imprisoned. I gave an experimental tug, and Rafe gripped a little tighter.

"I just want to touch you." I spoke on a shudder breath as he moved his mouth to the other sensitive tip, sucking gently and then blowing against the wet cloth until I shivered.

"No. This time, you're not in control. You're not getting your own way." The rumble of his voice against my nipple made me writhe.

"Harder. Please. Suck harder." I had no shame about saying what I wanted. There was no thought, no reason, just my body and everything I was feeling.

Rafe laughed softly as he raised his mouth to my ear. "Ah, Nell. Even with your hands out of commission, so turned on you can barely breathe, you're still trying to tell me what to do." He sucked the lobe into his mouth, tongued it. "Relax, baby. Just ... be."

His hand swept down the front of my shirt and over my stomach, inching under the waistband of my shorts. I tilted my hips to make it easier for him to reach me.

Fumbling with the buttons and zipper, he tugged the shorts down, just far enough that he could slip his fingers into my underwear and stroke my hot, wet center.

I had been so ready, wanting this for so long, that the minute I felt the light pressure of his hands on me, my hips pumped and my vision exploded as I climaxed. Rafe didn't stop his movements. He slid two fingers inside me, pumping in time with the spasms that were consuming me.

I sagged against the wall, and if Rafe's hand hadn't been holding me up, I'm sure I would have melted into a molten puddle on the floor. Instead, he covered my lips again, this kiss gentler, although just as intense. He pulled his hand out of my shorts and released my wrists, kneeling to catch me at the knees and cradle me in his arms, never breaking the kiss.

He carried me to the bed and laid me down, and then moved his lips to kiss my forehead.

"Stay here," he whispered. "I'll be right back."

I couldn't have moved if my life had depended on it. I heard him in the other room, and then I felt him come back to me. His energy was so strong that I could sense him even if we weren't touching. The bed dipped on the other side, and his hand skimmed down to my hip.

"Are you awake?" He nuzzled my neck.

"I think I am. Unless that was a dream."

He laughed, his breath ticking my collarbone. "Not unless we're both dreaming."

I opened one eye and turned my head a little. He had shed his clothes, and the sight of his tanned body lying alongside my small white one gave me a new burst of energy.

"Am I allowed to touch now?" I raised a hand to his shoulder.

"Not only allowed, but encouraged." He reached for the hem of my shirt. "But you seem to be a little overdressed. Can I help you remedy that?"

I lifted so that he could pull the shirt over my head. "Absolutely."

He tossed it to the floor and gazed down at my body, his eyes burning. He traced circles around each nipple until they both stood, aching and needing for his assault. He drew my breast into his mouth again.

"God, Nell, you are so beautiful. So perfect. Like porcelain." Still sucking on the stiff peak, he eased my shorts further down my legs, until I could kick them off.

"I want to take my time." He spoke against my skin as he circled his tongue around the other nipple. "But I've wanted you so much ... I'm not sure I can wait."

I smiled, smoothing my fingers down over the flat plains of his stomach to where his swollen cock rested against my hip. When I gripped him, moving my hand up and down languorously, Rafe groaned.

"And if you do that, it'll be even faster."

I laughed softly, rubbing the head with my thumb, using just enough pressure make him pant. He was exactly as I had dreamt, and then some: velvet-covered steel that heated and grew the more I moved my hand.

He responded by returning his hand to my pulsing core, caressing in time with my movements on his length. He circled one finger around the stiff bud of nerves, teasing, and then slipped his fingers within me. Everything in me centered on where his fingers were, on how they moved on me. He explored, opening and setting my body on fire with his tantalizing caress. His fingers found the right spot inside me and rubbed until I was ready to cry with need. Each time I thought I was coming near the edge, he eased me down, soothing my heated flesh.

Rafe kissed my neck, up to trace his tongue around my ear. "Nell, I want to be inside of you. I'm going to be part of you, as deep within as your soul. When I sink into you, there won't be a part of your body that doesn't touch me. I want to feel you tight and wet around me. I'm going to make you come until you can't breathe."

I gripped his hips, urging him forward. "What are you waiting for?"

He sat up and reached to the night table. I watched in surprise as he rolled a condom over himself.

"Where did you ... ?" I began, but he positioned himself over me, the head of his cock nudging at my entrance, and he covered my lips again in a mind-numbing kiss.

"Tell you later. No talking now."

He held himself above me, staring down at me, his eyes dark and intense. He watched me, never breaking the gaze, as he filled me, pushing into me, until I felt unbearably stretched and teetering at the edge of ecstasy. When my eyes drifted closed, he laid his hand on my cheek.

"No, Nell. Open your eyes. I want to see you while I'm inside you. I want to watch you come, and I want you to see me, too. When I come inside you, I want you to know this is only you, and only me. No one else. Just us."

I looked at him, my eyes wide. *Only him, only me. Just us.*

Buried fully between my legs, he held my wrists and raised them over my head again to pin them down to the pillow.

"This worked well before."

I arched my hips, needing him to move, to take me hard and fast. Rafe didn't require persuasion; he pulled out almost all the way and then rocked his hips to plunge back into me.

"Look at me, Nell."

"I am." I kept my eyes locked on his, as he moved faster, sinking into me further with each motion, until I felt pleasure build to an almost unbearable release. The entire world shrunk to the sensation of him, between my legs, my ankles locked behind his back, urging him closer, harder, faster.

I moaned his name, loud and long, and my orgasm, gripping him from within, pushed him over the edge.

His body tensed into one long quiver, but he never closed his eyes.

"Nell." He ground out my name, and I felt tears spring to my eyes at the mix of passion and unexpected tenderness.

He collapsed onto me, his face in the crook of my neck, and I knew without a doubt that this was the best moment of my life.

CHAPTER 18

I OPENED MY EYES to the unfamiliar feeling of lips on my stomach. Rafe's dark head was resting between my breasts, his mouth moving over my skin. I thrilled to the roughness of his day-old beard chafing against me.

Gladness rushed into fill me. I had drifted off to sleep, terrified that Rafe would regret this, that he would laugh at me. But evidence of that he wanted me again was pressing against my leg, and I smiled, lifting my hand to thread my fingers through his hair.

He turned his head to look up at me, meeting my smile with his own. "Do you know, that's when I first realized I wanted you? When you cut my hair. Every time you touched me, I wanted to grab you. And when I opened my eyes and you were right there in front of me ..." He palmed one breast. "I wanted to do this." He captured the tip with his lips and tongue, lazily sucking.

I arched and held his head in place. "God, that feels incredible."

"You are beautiful and perfect, Nell. More lovely than I

could have imagined."

I felt heat flood my face. "I'm small."

"Perfect," Rafe insisted. "Absolutely and completely perfect."

He shifted up onto his elbows, reaching for the nightstand again.

"Wait a minute. I want to know now. Where did the condoms come from? Please don't tell me you found them here at the cabin."

He laughed. "No. I bought them when we went into town last time."

I frowned. "When? And why?"

"When you were in the restroom. And why. . I would think that would be obvious."

"You were planning to do this that long ago?"

"Longer than that, though I was ... conflicted. I wouldn't say I planned anything. I just felt like it was a good idea to be prepared. Nell, I didn't want to want you. It's why I keep pushing you away."

I frowned. "Thanks."

"No, it's not you. It's what I told you before. I felt guilty, like if I was with you, it would make my time with Joss somehow ... less. When we talked the other day, and I told you about her, I realized you were right. She would want me to go on living, and this is part of living." He picked up a strand of my hair and curled it around his finger. "As a matter of fact, she'd be damned pissed at me for taking this long to make my move. Joss was very passionate. Very physical."

I turned my face away a little so Rafe couldn't see me. He reached up, touching my chin with his finger and forcing me to turn back.

"Hey, what's wrong?"

I sighed. "Rafe, I know I come across strong and in charge. I know people see me as an uber-bitch. And that's fine. But I have insecurities, too, and hearing the man in bed with me talk about how hot his girlfriend was isn't one of my fantasies." I rolled away again, burying my face in the pillow. Doubts and questions flooded my mind. I could never be Joss. I was only Nell, broken and crazy, the one people always left.

Pain morphed into power, and the room began to tremble. The headboard of the bed rattled against the wall. I tried to pull it back, but the hurt had blossomed, and I couldn't make it go away.

"Nell—" Rafe struggled to sit up more, but before he could get out of the way, a cup on the tilting nightstand tipped over, dumping ice-cold water over his head.

I stared, wide-eyed, as he sprang up, spraying water everywhere when he shook his head. With one last measure of concentration, I clamped down on the wild energy, stilling the cabin and leaving us in sudden quiet.

I waited for Rafe to be angry. "I'm sorry. I just ..." I threw an arm over my eyes. "I told you. I'm dangerous to have around."

Rafe laughed and used the edge of the sheet to wipe off his face. "I don't know. Usually when I say I want to rattle the headboard, that's not what I mean."

When I only groaned and pulled the pillow up over my face, he tugged it out of my hands and sat next to me on the bed. "I'm sorry. That was bad timing, talking about Joss. What can I say, I'm a guy." He moved up to lie between my legs, holding my face in his two hands. "But trust me, Nell.

I'm not comparing. I want to be open with you, and part of that is going to be talking about Joss. She was important. She mattered. Hell, if it weren't for her, I wouldn't be here in bed with you right now."

"I'm not asking for a confession of love, Rafe." I shut my eyes. "I know who I am. I'm not Tasmyn and I'm not Joss. I'm a fucked-up mess, and I don't do *this*." I pointed to him and then back to myself, finally opening my eyes again. "Sex to me has always been about power. Getting more, keeping it for myself. I was sixteen when I decided it was time to lose my virginity. I found someone who seemed like a good candidate, and I made it happen. And after that, I used sex when I had to. But never without planning out how I could manipulate the situation, gain the upper hand."

"And just how does having sex with me give you the upper hand?" Rafe watched me, no condemnation or judgment.

"It doesn't. Or at least I can't see how it does. There must be something else going on. Some kind of magical bond. Something in our touch that makes you want me."

His brows drew together. "Why do you say that?"

"Because why else would you sleep with me? I don't have anything to offer, except I'm convenient. I'm here." I turned my head again, this time determined to hide my own pain.

Rafe traced the shell of my ear with the tip of his finger. "Nell, I don't know what's between us yet. But it's not just the magic, though I think there's a component of that. And it's sure as hell not convenience. Take my word for it. You're damned inconvenient. I didn't want to care for another woman ever. When I look at you, I don't see someone who happens to be in the right place at the right time. I see a strong and stubborn woman who makes me hard just by walking into the kitchen or yelling at me when I make her mad."

He slid his mouth along my cheek to my mouth and kissed the corner of my lips. "And speaking of being hard ..." This time when he leaned to the nightstand for a condom, I didn't stop him. I folded my arm beneath my head, watching him roll the rubber over his stiff cock. It made me ache within.

He rose onto his knees and looked down at me, wearing the half-smile that set me on fire. "Trust me on this, too. You have nothing to be insecure about. Not one thing."

Rafe cupped my breast in one hand, rolling the nipple between his finger and thumb. His mouth fastened on the other side, sucking hard until I moaned.

"You like it a little rougher here, don't you?" he murmured.

"Mmmmm." I wriggled, running my nails lightly up and down his back. "Just don't stop."

He smiled against me. "I'll only stop when I find something even better to do with my mouth."

I think I died a little.

For a full day, Rafe and I didn't talk about going back to Florida. We stayed in bed the rest of the afternoon, alternating between making love (although I only called it that in my head) and sleeping. When it got dark, Rafe pulled one of his large t-shirts over my head and dragged me into the kitchen to sit with him while he made us dinner.

"I like knowing you're sitting there in my shirt, with nothing at all on underneath." He stopped on his way to the stove, tilted my head up and kissed me, stroking the inside of my lips with his tongue.

"As long as you're cooking, I'll sit here naked."

We ate, and then I did the dishes, while Rafe stood behind me, my back to his chest. He lazily played with my breasts until I was panting, and then reached under the shirt, between my legs to finish me off, his fingers unrelenting against my wet and swollen flesh as I leaned over the sink. While I was still gasping and jelly-legged, he scooped me up and carried me back to bed.

"I can't get enough of you." He growled the words down my neck, dropping me onto the mattress. "Each time I think I'm empty, you look at me ... and I'm fucking hard again."

Rafe's words made me feel powerful in a way I'd never experienced. It was a different kind of control, the ability to bring him to his knees with want. As he held his body over mine, his lips sucking at mine, kissing and ravishing, I gripped his hips and flipped us over.

This I was used to: being the one to call the shots in bed as well as out was how I did sex up to now. But even straddling Rafe, looking down into his desire-glazed eyes, felt new.

I leaned forward, letting my breasts graze his hard chest. Rewarded with his quick suck in of air, I smiled and leaned close to his ear.

"And now you're mine. What shall I do with you?"

"Just don't turn me into a frog." His voice was rough

with passion.

"A frog wouldn't be much use to me right now." I reached between us and wrapped my fingers around his length, already hard. "But this ... this I can work with."

Sliding down his body, I rubbed the apex of my legs over his thigh, moaning at the sensation. I wanted to stop there, ride his leg as his firm muscles rubbed into my wet core. But I had other things in mind. I lay flat on top of him, my mouth trailing kissed down his stomach until I reached my own hands, still holding his erection.

"Nell ... oh my God. So good."

I ran my tongue along one side of his pulsing arousal. "And about to get even better." I took him into my mouth, just the head at first, circling my tongue a few times, and then I lowered until my lips surrounded his base. I sucked lightly as I moved upward, gripping him with my fingers.

Rafe's hands knotted in my hair, encouraging, not forcing. I increased my tempo a little at a time, reveling in the feel of him in my mouth, touching the back of my throat.

"Nell." His fingers urged me up. "I want to come inside you. I want to see your face."

I licked one last time and then pulled myself back along his body. "This is my game. I'm in control now."

He grinned, cupping my cheek in his hand. "I'm all for that. Have me as you will."

"Lucky for you, I want you this way." I fumbled for another condom and tore open the packet. Keeping my eyes on Rafe's, I slowly rolled it over him, humming in appreciation as I did.

"You're killing me." He sounded strangled.

"But what a way to go." Never looking away from his

face, I poised my entrance over his swollen manhood and sank, pulling him deep within my hot, tight sheath.

Rafe's eyes rolled up and closed. I shifted, leaning forward, and picked up one of his hands. Placing it on my breast, I touched his cheek.

"Look at me. Know that this is me you're inside. I'm the one riding you." His fingers closed over my puckered nipple. "I'm going to make you come so hard."

I rose up until he was nearly out of me and then plunged over again, finding my rhythm and what movement brought us both the most pleasure. I undulated my hips, crying out when he rubbed against the spot of nerves inside me.

"Nell ... oh, God. Nell."

Lost to anything but my own pleasure, I arched back and ground into him until I shattered, crying out and tightening in spasms around his cock. Rafe held my shoulders and bucked upwards, shouting my name as he came.

I woke in the middle of the night, in the dark, wrapped in his arms. I glanced down at his hands, liberally sprinkled with black hair, crossed over my breasts, and thought that everything else that had ever happened in my life was worth it, if that was what it took to get me here, now. Even if this only lasted a day, I would hold onto this memory forever.

Rafe made me breakfast in bed the next morning, kissing me on the nose as he placed the cookie sheet that served as a serving tray on my lap. He amused me with stories about his grandparents as we ate. He spoke of them with such obvious affection that I found myself a little envious.

"I remember my grandmothers. My mom's mother died before my mom went away. I always thought that if she were still alive, maybe she would have taken me. Maybe things would have turned out differently."

"Hey." Rafe drew my lips to his. "Everything happens for a reason. I know your childhood sucked, but I'm glad you survived it to be here. If you didn't, I'd be six feet under in Georgia clay."

I smiled and reached for his hand. I pressed our palms together and wove my fingers between his. "The spark when we touch ... tell me how it makes you feel."

Rafe pulled our linked hands to his mouth and kissed my fingers. "From the first, it felt ... sexual. Like I needed to be close to you, as close as I could get. And electric, like my whole body was one big nerve. And powerful."

"Mmmm." I lay back, stretching. "Exactly."

Rafe drew circles on the back of my hand with his tongue, and I smiled, my eyes drifting shut.

"Nell."

"Mmmhmm."

"I still want to talk about what happens when we go back to Florida." He shifted to lie alongside me. "We go together, as a team. No more talk about you running off and living in the wilderness, okay?"

I sighed. "Rafe ... I don't know. I like your optimism. But everything I said yesterday is still true."

"But now you have me. You know I won't leave you. You won't be alone."

I opened my eyes and looked into Rafe's face. I traced his lips with the tip of my finger. Didn't he know that was what they all said, in the beginning?

"You say that now. Once we're back, things could be different. If they are, I won't hold you to anything."

"Nell, for God's sake. Give me a little credit, please."

"I don't think it's that unreasonable to assume that when we're back in our normal lives, you're going to wonder what you ever saw in me."

Rafe sighed and dropped his forehead to lean against my shoulder. "Will you think about it? Give it a try?"

"Okay." There was something about this boy that made me want to trust him, even when I knew deep down this would never work. "I'll try it."

His smile was brilliant. "Good. That's all I ask."

After breakfast, Rafe convinced me that we needed to get out of the cabin. We had seen flyers for the weekly farmers market when we were in town, and he wanted to send another text to Carruthers. It was safer to do that away from the cabin than in it.

The market was on the town green, a space smaller than a football field. Rafe and I wandered from table to stall, tasting honey, eating samples of freshly baked bread and checking out the vegetables.

A small booth next to the homemade soap booth caught my eye. The woman was elderly, dressed in faded overalls, a plaid shirt and a straw hat. The table in front of her was spread with jewelry.

"Good morning," she greeted us as we passed. "Aren't you a beautiful couple?"

I flushed; I wasn't sure what Rafe would think of us being labeled a couple when he hadn't made his feelings for me clear yet. But he just pulled me tight against his side and smiled.

"Well, *she's* beautiful." He kissed the top of my head. "I'm just an appreciator."

I leaned to examine a sterling silver necklace. "You have lovely things here."

She grinned. "And they're not just pretty to look at. Each and every piece has meaning. I travel around the world collecting the most unique jewelry."

I held my hand over the necklace, and immediately I felt a sense of foreboding. I pulled away.

"Where did that come from?"

The woman smiled at me, her lips thin. "A village in Romania. It's enchanted. You feel the power, I can see. Well, don't worry. It's not cursed or anything, I don't deal in that. But it's not for you."

I raised an eyebrow and glanced at Rafe. He shrugged.

"Now for you ..." She regarded me, cocking her head. "Yes, just as I thought. It's been waiting for you."

She reached below the table and produced a gleaming wooden box. "Try this."

I opened the box. Inside, nestled in ancient and worn red velvet, was a delicate silver and onyx bracelet. I gasped in wonder before I could stop myself. Rafe took the box from me and fastened the bracelet on my wrist.

"See? Like it was made for you." She smiled from one of us to the other.

"We'll take it." Rafe nudged me. "You have the money."

"How much?" I asked, digging in my pocket.

"This is a bracelet that was meant to live on your arm, my dear. I didn't put it out today, because when I bought it,

I was told the right owner would find it. And you did. I would give it to you outright, but it's meant to be a gift from your lover, not from me. So, we'll say twenty dollars."

I smoothed out a twenty and handed it to Rafe with a smirk. "So you can pay."

The woman took the money from him, holding onto his hand for a beat longer than necessary.

"Blessings, my dears." She looked at us both. "Wear it in health."

We drove as far out of town as possible, in the opposite direction of the cabin, to text Cathryn. Rafe turned onto the shoulder of the road near a farm and pulled out the phone. He punched the number I recited and sent the simple question mark text.

We waited, both jittery and tense. I watched the time click down on the phone's clock until all five minutes has passed without a response.

"Damn." Rafe smacked the steering wheel. "What's going on out there, that we can't go back home? Sitting around here waiting ..." His jaw clenched.

I tried to hide my own relief. "If she's not calling us back, there's a reason for it. Cathryn is cautious, that's all."

He scowled. "But we know more than she does." He picked up the phone again, staring at the screen. "I'm going to call her."

"Rafe, she told us what to do."

"No, she told *you*. But the situation is different now.

We'll be careful. We're away from the cabin, and we'll toss the phone as soon as we're done."

Before I could argue again, Rafe pressed in the numbers and hit send. I fold my hands tightly in my lap, hoping that this wasn't a mistake. We both sat stiffly, scanning our surroundings as the phone rang on the other end.

Finally, I heard a click and a cautious female voice answered. *Cathryn.*

"Hello?"

Rafe cleared his throat. "This is Rafe Brooks."

There was an exclamation on the other end of the line. "Oh, thank God. Thank God. Rafe, we won't use other names on this line, since it's not secure, but do you know who this is?"

He nodded as though she could see him. "Yeah. Pocket–sized boss lady."

Her laughter ended on a near-sob. "Yes, that's right. Are you with ... someone else we both know?"

He smiled at me. "I am, and we want to know if it's safe to come in."

"No. We're on the verge of a big movement with—that assignment. You shouldn't have called today. We need to end this call. Don't give me any other information. Forces working against us are still at large, and you need to use caution. Understood?"

"It's my middle name."

She sighed. "Rafe, please. You need to stay away, for just a little longer. I'm hanging up now. Destroy the phone."

"But—" Rafe gritted his teeth. "Okay. Fine. Will do."

He disconnected the call, and for a moment, he just sat, looking down at his lap. After a minute, he climbed out of the car and dropped the phone on the asphalt. He crushed it with his heel and flung two of the pieces into a nearby field. The others he put in his pocket to toss as we drove.

The Impala could move fast when the right person was driving her, and Rafe didn't let up on the pedal all the way back to the cabin. He didn't speak, and I sat silent in the passenger seat.

When we stopped in from of the cabin, he turned to look at me.

"Nell, I don't care what Cathryn says. We need to go back. We'll be careful, and we'll be smart, but we're going home. If something's going down with this fight, I sure as hell don't plan to be sitting on the sidelines."

I stared into the trees. I knew there was nothing I could say to change his mind. And if we were walking into a huge mistake, the least I could do was walk with him until he didn't want me anymore.

I forced a smile onto my lips and took his face between my hands.

"Okay, Rafe. We'll go home."

CHAPTER
19

FOUR DAYS LATER, WE left the cabin.

I didn't want to go. If I truly was a person who got her own way all the time, Rafe and I would have stayed in that cabin, by ourselves, for the rest of our lives. I would have lived in grateful contentment, asking for nothing else.

But I knew Rafe needed to go back. He had to assure his grandparents that he was alive and well, and he wanted to be part of ending Mallory Jones and her Hive once and for all.

Rafe seemed to know how I felt about leaving, though. He was kind to me those last days, even as I could feel his growing anticipation of being back at Carruthers. We made love each night, but it was beginning to feel like goodbye to me. Even so, Rafe stayed close, pulling me into his arms at random moments; I fought the temptation to push him away in preparation for the hurt I knew was inevitable once we got back to Florida.

We had decided to depart after midnight, just as I had when I left Carruthers back in June. As dusk fell on our last night, I sat on the porch, trying desperately to absorb the peace in this place.

"Howdy, Miss Nell."

My face broke into a smile at the familiar voice. "Doc! Oh, I'm so glad to see you. Where have you been?" We hadn't seen him since his last check-in on Rafe after the pneumonia.

"Oh, out and about, here and there. Seems there's still some who can use an old geezer like me now and then. Good to know I'm not quite put out to pasture yet."

I leaned my chin on the railing of the porch, looking down at Doc. "Can you come in? Have a cup of tea?"

"I wish I could, my dear, but I've got tasks awaiting me, and so do you."

I cocked my head. "What do you mean?"

He nodded toward the Impala. The backseat was packed with grocery bags and the clothes we'd bought while living here.

"Looks like you're moving on."

I heaved a sigh. "Yes, we are."

"You're not ready?"

I lifted a shoulder. "Does it matter if I am or not? Rafe's itching to go. And he's right. If we stay here, we'll just be hiding from ... life. Not living it."

"Good to hear that boy picked up some sense somewhere." He winked at me. "And you, Miss Nell. You're different, too."

I smiled again. *Oh, boy, was I.*

"Really? How so?"

Doc grinned. "You found peace. You're calm." He took two steps forward and reached up to the pat my arm. "Have faith, dear one. All is as it's meant to be."

A shiver ran up my spine. I trusted Dr. Eli. He had saved Rafe's life, and if he were connected with Mallory's group, he had had ample opportunity to turn us in and hadn't. Besides, he was surrounded with an air of rightness. But still, I wasn't entirely sure he was who he said he was.

As if he could read my mind, Doc sighed. "So much darkness in the world. It's not surprising most of us are suspicious of those who come to help. But you needn't. Every now and then, we're sent a little light for the path. Someone to ease our burden at just the right time. When that happens, the best thing to do is to be grateful. Not all questions have to be answered, after all."

"Thank you, Doc." I stood up and ran lightly down the porch steps. I hesitated only a moment before I clasped the old man in a hug.

"No, Nell dear, thank *you*." He patted my back. "Now, I have to be moving on. Safe travels. Give that young man of yours my best."

Doc moved back to the path. I heard his whistled song long after he had vanished into the night.

"Who were you talking to?" Rafe came through the screen door.

"Doc. He just passed through. I think he stopped to say good-bye."

He frowned. "How did he know we were leaving?"

I shook my head. "I have no idea. Maybe he didn't. But he knows now because he saw the car. He told me to give you his best."

Rafe nodded. "Odd old man. Did you tell him we looked for his cabin?"

"No, it didn't seem to matter. We probably just didn't

go far enough when we walked down the path." I thought of what he'd told me about being grateful. "Let's just be happy he was here when we needed him."

"Still." We sat in silence for a few minutes, and then Rafe slid down to sit next to me on the swing. He draped his arm around my shoulders and pulled me to his side.

"I know you don't want to leave. Thank you for doing it anyway."

I laid my head on his shoulder. "You're welcome. Will we come back someday, do you think?" I was opening myself up to hurt by asking that question, I knew; it spoke to a future we hadn't yet discussed.

"I promise, if we get through this fight, we'll come back." He reached across my lap to take my hand in his. "We'll come back, and you can throw me off the porch for old time's sake, okay?"

I rolled my eyes and swatted at him. "Watch it. I'll knock you off tonight just for the hell of it."

He chuckled. "Got it."

I closed my eyes and wished that time would stop. It wasn't only leaving the cabin or going back to Florida. I knew that we were going back to war. To danger and the loss of friends and possible death.

Thinking of it, out of habit I did my usual sweep of the area for extraordinary minds. It was the typical blank ... until ...

"Rafe." I whispered his name, though I didn't think whoever it was could be that close. "Someone's near."

He tensed. "Who?"

"I don't know. Someone with power." I probed again, trying to get more specifics. "Not on the mountain, but close.

Maybe ... circling."

"Shit." Rafe tightened his arm around me. "We've been here for months, and now, the night we leave, someone decides to bother us? It can't be coincidence."

"What should we do?" I glanced at the car. "Should we leave?"

"We're going to have to. Up here, we're sitting ducks if they know where we are. We'll go inside, I'll get the cooler and then we'll hit the road. But we can't go directly back to—" He glanced around. "Where we were going. I won't lead anyone back to them, if they don't already know."

A horrific mental image flew across my mind, of Harper Creek, that beautiful, stately home, wrecked and burning, with bodies everywhere. *Payback for Georgia.*

I steadied my breath. I didn't have visions; I wasn't a precog. That was just my overactive imagination. It was fear, and it was dread. It hadn't happened, and by God, it wouldn't. I wouldn't let it happen.

I sat up, easing away from Rafe's side. "Okay. I'll get my last minute things together, and you work on the cooler."

"Nell." Rafe caught my arm. "It's going to be okay. This is just a little blip."

I leaned in to kiss him, as much for my own comfort as to thank him. As I did, I heard an odd rustle in the bushes just beyond the path.

"Well, talk about surprise. Rafe Brooks and Nell Massler. Two of my favorite people from King, Florida. Fancy running into you here."

CHAPTER
2⊕

I KNEW THE VOICE, but I couldn't place it right away. And before I could turn around, Rafe gripped my arm. He stood, putting his body in front of me so that I was hidden.

"Cara. What the hell are you doing here?"

Of course, Cara Pryce. The girl from King who, with her pastor father, had saved Tasmyn from my plan to let a little blood. The same girl I'd seen in June, tossing food and water down to Rafe in his hole.

I had to say, Cara had seen better days. She'd never been an especially pretty girl; nothing about her stood out. But now she was painfully bone-thin, and her hair had been hacked off at the chin. It was dirty. She wore torn jeans and a flannel shirt that was several sizes too big.

"I'm here to warn you." She answered Rafe's question, but the whole time, she never stopped looking around, over her shoulder and beyond us.

"Oh, really? Forgive me if I don't believe you, Cara, but the last time we hung out, your friends tried to kill me. They did kill Joss. And then they tossed me down in a hole for months."

"It was because of me that they didn't kill you. I brought you food and water, didn't I?" She hooked a thumb at her own chest.

"Yeah, you tossed me down some supplies, I'll give you that. But they were going to murder me anyway. The only reason I'm still alive is because Nell saved me."

Her eyes shifted to me. "And what is King's favorite psycho doing out in the world? Got some blood rituals to perform? Witchcraft?" She waved her fingers in the air.

"Cara, we don't have time to screw around here. Why are you warning us? And how did you find us?" Rafe tightened his grip on me. I wondered if he worried I might get pissed and do something to Cara. He didn't know that this girl had always flown under my radar. She wasn't worth expending the energy.

"Mallory has people looking for you. She has, ever since Georgia. What happened that day, anyway?"

Rafe clenched his jaw. "No time for that. Just tell me. Did you lead them here?"

She shook her head. "No, I didn't lead them here. It was the other way around. They blamed me for what happened in Georgia. Mallory thought I had tipped off someone— whoever it was who destroyed the camp—about Rafe being there. But Nathan begged her not to kill me. And I guess she got orders from the queen, too. So I got to live, but not like before. They kept me in a house, tied up, wherever we went."

"So where have you been all this time?" Rafe's tone was hostile. He didn't like this chick at all.

She shrugged. "They've been moving me around from camp to camp. None of the big ones, just little drone colonies. Early last week, they sent me to one a little west of here. About a hundred miles away."

I looked at Rafe, my heart in my throat. *All this time, Mallory had a camp that close to us ...*

"I got there, and I overheard them talking about you. About Rafe and some girl who was with him. I didn't know it was you." She raised her eyebrows at me. "Anyway, they had you tracked close to here, and they're sending someone in tonight."

I was the girl who wasn't afraid of anything. I had to remind myself of that. But right now, the idea that Mallory or one of her henchmen was closing in on us, putting Rafe in danger ... yup. I was pretty sure that was fear.

"And you're what, the welcoming committee?" Rafe spat the words at Cara. "Thanks for the warning."

"No!" Cara hissed at him. "You've got to believe me. They're close, but you can still get away. I slipped away from the camp the same night the tracker left. I hid in the back of the truck, and I got out the last time they stopped for gas. They're arrogant, and they get sloppy. And then they make mistakes. You have time."

"And just what's in it for you?" Rafe cocked an eyebrow.

"Take me with you. I want to go back to Pennsylvania. I want to go home." She hugged her arms around her thin torso. "I'm tired of this. I just want to be with my parents again." Her voice broke on a sob.

"Pennsylvania is a little out of our way." The tears didn't affect Rafe.

Cara took one step closer. "Rafe, one of the things Mallory and Nathan said was that you work for someone who's trying to stop the Hive. If that's true, I can tell you where the center of everything is. I know where they're planning to kick off the revolution. If you take me home, I'll tell you everything I know."

Rafe tensed, but he kept his voice casual. "And what makes you think I want to take down the Hive?"

Cara snorted. "Rafe, I'm not an idiot. I know you have some kind of ability. And I know you were in the camp in Georgia trying to stop us. Or them, rather. After you tried to leave and Mallory killed Joss, they were all trying to figure out who you work for. So I figure if you're some kind of secret agent, you'd be interested in knowing when the big bang's going to happen."

Rafe flipped up a hand. "So tell me."

"Happily." Cara smiled through her tears. "After we're in Pennsylvania."

"And how do we know this isn't a trap?"

"You don't. You have to trust me, Rafe, just a little, and I have to trust you, that you're not going to drive right to Washington and turn me in as a terrorist." She looked over her shoulder and lowered her voice. "I'm tired, Rafe. I just want to go home."

I saw the indecision in Rafe's eyes. He wanted that information, and he wanted to get us off the mountain before it was too late, but he couldn't be sure about Cara. I leaned forward to whisper in his ear.

"We have to do this. We'll watch her. But we don't have any choice."

He nodded, and I knew he'd been coming to that same conclusion himself.

"All right, Cara. Give us five minutes, then we're out of

here."

Cara sagged in relief. "Thank you. I promise, you won't be sorry."

Rafe whispered to me. "Go inside and get your stuff, and toss whatever we need in the cooler. I'm going to stand out here and keep my eye on her. I don't trust her inside."

I nodded and darted into the cabin. There wasn't time to sit and think about what we were about to do; we needed to move and move fast.

I grabbed my last bag from the bedroom, opened the cooler and dumped in the ice, the chicken Rafe had fried earlier in the day and some bottled waters. I carried both out to the porch.

"If you load them in the car, I'll turn off the generator and water."

Rafe picked up the cooler. "Deal. Meet you at the Impala in five."

When I returned, Cara was in the back seat and Rafe stood alongside the car. He watched me approach, and I saw brooding in his eyes.

He pulled me close for a minute. "I know what you're thinking. This is a disaster waiting to happen. But we have to get this information, if we're going to fry that Mallory bitch."

I squeezed his hand and walked around the car to my side. Our doors slammed, Rafe hit the accelerator, and we were gone. I glanced at the cabin in the rearview mirror.

Goodbye, peace. Hello, war.

We made it to the road at the base of the mountain without incident. I could still feel someone near us, but at least we'd avoided being trapped on the hill.

"Shit." Rafe hit the steering wheel with the heel of his hand. "We need gas. And if we don't get it now, we'll run out before we hit the highway."

I swallowed. "I don't think it's safe yet."

"We've got to do it. I'll be fast. Keep your eyes open and yell if you see anyone."

That didn't sound like the most foolproof plan, but it was what we had. Rafe circled around to the small town and found the discount store that had a rare twenty-four hour gas station.

He had just finished pumping the gas when a black sedan pulled in front of us. Power pulsed from the car. I yelled for Rafe, and he sprinted around to the driver's side of the Impala.

Two men got out of the other car and began to approach us. One held up his hand, and our car jerked, shaking.

"Block them, Nell." Rafe spoke through gritted teeth. "One's a manipulator."

"Not a problem." My mind guards were up anyway, and seeing these two didn't scare me. On the contrary, they made me angry.

I let out a little rage and pushed them back against their car. The second man was harder to move, but he fell back eventually.

"They're going to follow us, even if we slow them down." Rafe looked back at Cara, who sat silent and terrified in the back seat.

"No, I don't think so." Staring at the car, I opened both doors and pushed the men inside it. Then, concentrating harder, I flipped the locks and broke them. The doors couldn't be open from the inside anymore.

One last finishing touch, I decided. I popped the hood with my mind and focused on hoses, on pipes, on anything that might be essential to making a car run. Once steam was hissing from the engine, I smiled at Rafe.

"Let's go. Now."

Cara was not the most annoying passenger I'd ever known, much to my surprise. I'd expected her to rattle on about King or Tasmyn or me, but once we knew we had gotten away from the cabin and were not being followed, she fell asleep, leaving Rafe and me to talk in peace.

"How long is it going to take?" I smothered a yawn.

Rafe glanced over at me. "About eight hours, I think. But I'm estimating. Could be longer."

"I can drive if you get tired. Just let me know." I bit back another yawn, and Rafe laughed.

"I'm okay. I'm too wired to sleep right now anyway. Just close your eyes. If I need you, I'll let you know."

I glanced back at Cara. Her eyes were shut and her mouth sagged.

"What do you think we're going to find out? Is this a wild goose chase? A way for her to get a ride home?"

"I really don't know what to think." Rafe looked into his rearview mirror. "But we didn't have any options. And as much as I don't like her ..." He swiveled his eyes to the backseat. "... She did keep them from killing me in Georgia. At least long enough for you to get there."

"Mmm." I laid my head on the seat and my eyes drifted shut. "That was a good thing."

I felt Rafe reach over to squeeze my hand, and then I was asleep.

When I awoke, the pitch back night surrounded us still. Cara was snoring.

"Where are we?"

"Virginia." Rafe stretched his arms. "Can you do a sweep and make sure we're not being followed?"

I did. It was harder when we were moving, but I managed to get a good sense of who was around us.

"I'm not picking up anyone." I arched my back. "Want to pull off and switch?"

Rafe nodded. "Sure. I'm starting to get a little bleary-eyed."

I had been driving about two hours, with Rafe sound asleep in the seat next to me, when Cara woke up. She was quiet for a few minutes, and then she leaned forward.

"So, Nell. I heard you got put away in the crazy house. Did you escape?"

I gritted my teeth. "No. I was deemed healthy enough to exist in society, so they let me go." *Not quite truth, but close enough.*

"Do you ever hear from Tasmyn?" I knew Cara meant that as a jeer, but I turned it around.

"Yes, actually. She came to visit me in the hospital all the time." *I was in a coma, but you don't need to know that.*

Cara was taken aback. "Really?"

"Yes, really. You know she and Michael are going to school together at Perriman. They're talking marriage."

Cara's lips tightened, and I felt a petty joy. Cara had

always had a crush on Tasmyn's boyfriend.

"You know my dad always swore there was more to the scene in the forest than you trying to kill Tasmyn. He said she was a witch. That you both were. If you're such good buddies now, I guess maybe he wasn't wrong."

"Of course he wasn't." It was a partial lie, partial truth. "And the great thing about being a witch is that I could do anything to anyone, and I can't be stopped. People who annoy me find that out fast." I met her eyes in the rearview, giving her a meaningful glance. She retreated to her corner of the backset.

The rest of my drive was quiet.

We crossed the border into southeastern Pennsylvania in the early hours of the morning. Rafe was driving again by then, and he pulled into a well-lit gas station, put the car in park and turned around to face Cara.

"Okay. We're in Pennsylvania. I want to hear now what you know. All of it."

Cara nodded. "All right. There's a camp, just outside Gettysburg. It's big. After everything got destroyed at the one in Georgia, they changed their center of operations to this one. In three days, everything goes down. This is a prime location, with DC, Philly and even New York so close. They have drones planted in all those cities. Weapons sent in. And camps across the country—and the world—ready to move as soon as they get the sign."

"And the sign is?" Rafe's hands tightened on the steering wheel.

"The camp goes up in flames. A big, cult-like mass suicide of people setting themselves and each other on fire. The drones are sacrificial in this one. Once that hits the news, everything else goes down like dominoes."

"Drones?" I glanced from Cara to Rafe. "You used that word before. What are they?"

"Not what, who." Rafe grimaced. "Remember I told you, at the camp in Georgia, most of the people didn't have any special abilities. They were recruited to keep up the front of it being a commune, and then they were being slowly indoctrinated into the plans of the higher ups."

"They're cannon fodder." Cara shook her head. "I know that's terrible, but it's true. The drones are supposed to be the front lines, to take the greatest casualties before the real soldiers come in."

"Is Mallory Jones at this camp near Gettysburg?" A lump of dread had formed in my throat, but we needed to know.

"I'm not sure. Maybe, though I'd be surprised if she's there when everything goes down. But I do know this. Whoever is the head of this whole organization is at the camp right now. The queen of the Hive is here."

"Who is it?" Rafe twisted in his seat. "I heard of this queen—but is it a woman? Are they taking that idiotic bee analogy to the limit? Or is the leader Ben, or even Nathan?"

Cara winced. "Not Ben. At least, I don't think. I haven't seen Ben in a long time. I don't know what happened to him. Nathan's just a middle-level agent. He was in charge of the camp in Georgia, but that was it. He got hurt pretty badly when the lodge exploded." She shot me a look, as though I might feel guilty. Not hardly.

Rafe sighed. "Cara, how far away from home are you now?"

She met his eye in the mirror. "Lancaster. About an hour

from here. If you can't take me any further, I understand. I can probably hitch a ride."

Rafe turned the ignition. "No, I'm making sure you get safely home. And then, no offence, Cara, but I hope I never see you again."

CHAPTER
21

"I THINK THIS IS IT."

On the way to Lancaster, Rafe had grilled Cara about a more exact location of the camp outside Gettysburg. After we left her in front of a small white church with an adjoining house, we began the trip to Gettysburg. It was a beautiful drive on back roads past huge farms and over gently rolling hills. If I weren't afraid that we were heading to certain doom, I probably would have enjoyed it.

We drove through the quaint little town of Gettysburg itself and skirted the battlefield. Tall gray granite monuments peppered the land, and even though it was very early, already groups of people were meandering over the trails. Following Cara's directions, we continued past the tourist attractions back into large open areas of farms and orchards until we arrived at the crossroad she had given us. Rafe eased the Impala to the side of the road as I closed my eyes and did a scan.

"There's a high concentration of people with power. We're out in the middle of freaking nowhere. Sounds about right. What are we going to do?" My stomach was turning. "I can project in and check it out."

"We don't have much time." Rafe looked up at the sky, which was growing lighter by the minute. "If we want to catch them asleep, we need to move fast."

"Just give me a boost. I won't take long, and at least we won't be going in blind."

Rafe took both my hands, our palms pressing together and our fingers linked. I breathed deep and willed myself into the camp. Just as in Tennessee, the trip was instantaneous ... until I hit something hard that shoved my metaphysical body back. I came to the car with a groan.

"What happened?" Rafe released my hands and touched my hair. "Are you okay?"

I nodded. "I think they have a block of some sort. It felt like I ran into a brick wall."

Rafe ran a hand through his hair. "Shit. Well, that at least answers the question of whether or not we're in the right place. And if they have that kind of guard up, it tells me something big is in that camp."

"Then I think we should call for back up." I reached into my bag for one of the last burner phones. "We wait until Cathryn can send reinforcements, and we go in strong."

"What if we're too late by the time they get here?" Rafe's voice was bleak. "If the plan is mass suicide, and if it's sooner than later, like Cara thought, I can't sit here waiting for them to go up in flames." He frowned, and I could tell he was considering my suggestion. "Let's compromise. We'll call Cathryn, let her know where we are and what's happening. But meanwhile, we go in and see if we can do this ourselves, or at least keep them busy until the cavalry gets here."

I sighed. It wasn't the plan I wanted, but I had a feeling it was the only plan I was going to get. "So how do you want to do it?"

"We're going in guns blazing. Metaphorical guns, of course. I think we should use the same strategy you did in Georgia. It's early morning, no one is expecting any trouble. Wind, trees flying, earth tremors ..." He shrugged. "I don't know what else to do. No fire that we can't control, though. We don't want to play into their sign and accidentally knock down these dominoes. Set the whole damn plan in motion just by trying to stop it."

"I thought you didn't approve of my methods last time." I took his hand in both of mine, rubbing it between them, to take the sting out of my words.

"I don't approve of wholesale murder, like what Mallory Jones does, but we need to stop this mess. And if that means there are some casualties ... I don't like it, but I don't see another way."

"We need to find out who's running the Hive. If she's here—or he, whatever—like Cara said, we have to try to take him alive. That's the only way we'll find out how widespread it is. Cut off the head, sure, but we'll need to take down the body, too."

Rafe nodded. "That's the mission, then. Get in, distract and delay, find the leader. The queen." He pulled my hand to his mouth and kissed my fingers. "And no heroics in there. If something happens that I get taken down and you're still alive, I don't want you in a hole dying by degrees. You get away, no matter what's happening to me."

I gripped his hand. "You're not going down. Neither am

I. We have too much to do. I swear to God, Rafe, if you don't come out of this in one piece, I'll make you sorry." I smiled at him, my old Nell, cut-your-throat-and-take-your-blood smile. "I'm scarier than anything you're going to see in that camp."

Rafe shook his head. "You don't have to tell me. I'm just glad you're on my side."

I raised one eyebrow. "Today I am. But you never can tell with a psycho bitch, can you? Just don't piss me off by getting hurt again. There's probably a limit to how many times I'll nurse you back to health."

"I'll keep that in mind."

Rafe telephoned Cathryn from the car, giving her as much information as he could in a short period of time.

"She's not happy with us." We were whispering as we made our way to the camp on foot.

"I'm not surprised. But she'll alert the authorities?"

"Yes, she has some bigwig on standby, once we let her know we have the leader. We don't want any of the people with abilities falling into government hands. Talk about out of frying pan, into the fire. Carruthers will restrain them and take them into custody."

This camp was bigger than the one in Georgia. We passed a few groupings of tents, but nothing that made me think we were near the headquarters. A few people were up, moving around in the early morning light. I had an odd sense of déjà vu, and I wondered if any of these people were refugees from the Georgia camp. Talk about bad luck.

I was about to say as much to Rafe when a shadow fell in front of me and a tall, thin man stepped out of the trees.

"Visitors." He looked from Rafe to me, grinning in a way that let me know he wasn't pulling around the Welcome Wagon for us. "Perfect timing. You folks come for a front seat to the biggest show around?"

I reached with my mind for a branch, a rock, anything to knock this guy out of way. But nothing budged. He just laughed as I struggled against the bindings I could feel around my powers.

"They're doing something bigger than a block." Rafe spoke through clenched teeth. "I can't do anything."

"We learned a thing or two from your last visit to one of our camps." The tall man grabbed my arm. "Come on, let's go. We've been expecting you. I have orders to bring you to the queen."

Rafe growled low in his throat as I was jerked forward, but there was nothing either of us could do. I ducked to avoid low branches and tried to keep from stumbling. Rafe kept up behind me.

"At least we'll find out who this queen is," I muttered when he was close to me. "Saves us a little time."

He didn't answer, and from the expression on his face, I could tell he was bracing himself for the worst.

But my captor laughed again as he pulled me into a small clearing.

"You want to know who's running this show? Happy to oblige." He pointed in front of us at a small structure, a hut of some sort. There was a crude doorway, but no door, only a dirty blanket hanging in the space. Another man stood alongside the makeshift opening, and he jumped to alertness when he spotted the three of us.

"Tell the queen her guests are here, Malcolm."

Malcolm leaned inside to speak and then stepped out of the doorway. My heart began to pound as a shadow fell over the ground behind him. I moved in front of Rafe. If Mallory Jones came through that door, by God she was in for a fight before she struck us down dead.

But it was not Mallory Jones who stepped through. The woman who appeared met my shocked eyes with a warm smile.

"Hello, Nell. I've been expecting you."

Once when I was a little girl, I went to a birthday party at a friend's house. It was after my mother had left, and I wasn't often invited to parties anymore. These people weren't native King residents, and they had a pool. Since I knew how to dive, I was a minor celebrity, which was a welcome relief from the notoriety I'd been dealing with since I was seven.

I stood on the diving board, looking down on the upturned faces of my classmates as they watched me prepared to execute a dive I'd been bragging I could do. I had the right form and a good takeoff, but something happened between the board and the water. Instead of sluicing into the water, I hit it square with my stomach—a classic belly flop.

I didn't know what was worse: the mortification over

completely messing up on my dive, or the way it felt like I couldn't breathe for long, excruciating moments afterwards.

Standing in the camp, looking at the woman in the doorway, I had that same sensation. No matter how much I tried to gasp, to take in air, my lungs were paralyzed, and I was suffocating.

When I could speak, it was only a squeak.

"Mama."

She moved forward with the same fluid grace I remembered from my childhood. Even the smile was the same. Her hair, identical to my own black curls, didn't show even a hint of gray. I noticed a few lines around her eyes, but other than that, she could have walked out of any of my memories from thirteen years ago.

"Darling, I'm so glad you finally found me." She drew me close, and the man holding my arm let go of me so that I could clutch her back.

She smelled the same. I had forgotten the unique scent my mother carried with her but now, surrounded by it again, I remembered.

"What are you doing here?" I could only whisper. My voice hadn't recovered yet.

"Haven't you guessed, Nell? This—all of this—is mine. I started it, I run it. It was my idea, and once everything falls into place, as it will, I'm going to rule the world."

"I thought you were in a hospital."

She nodded. "I thought you were, too."

"I was released."

She smirked. "I wasn't. I left of my own accord. With a little help."

"Does Daddy know?"

The smirk turned into a sneer. "Hardly. Someone else is there in my place, and if anyone checks to make sure I'm where I should be, they only see what I intend. But I doubt anyone checks. Your father hasn't concerned himself about either of us for a long time, Nell. He kept us apart, thinking he could keep the inevitable from happening. But we thwarted him, as I knew we would."

I frowned. "The inevitable? And what do you mean, he kept us apart?"

"Nell, you've been lied to for years. I was never the person your father told you I was. He was afraid of my power, and of the gifts I was passing down to you. He knew that together, you and I would be unstoppable. So he set me up. He wanted an excuse to leave us anyway, so it all worked out. Accused me of attempted murder, got me committed. Suddenly he was a free man, and he didn't have to worry about an inconvenient wife anymore."

My mind was swimming. *Was she telling me the truth?* My father had never spoken to me about my mother, but I knew it was true that he hated King. He hated what I could do.

"And he tried to do the same to you, when your power manifested. But you beat him, too, Nell! And now we're together. I've been waiting for you to join me. When Nathan told me who had destroyed the camp in Georgia ... well, it was an annoyance, yes, but I knew it was you, and it was just a matter of time until you found me."

"But you can't do this." The shock was beginning to give way to logic. If my mother was in charge here, did that make her a bad person? Was she the evil leader Rafe and I had been planning to capture?

"Oh, I most certainly can. And you can, too. Come, Nell. You know you've always had these leanings. I heard about your adventures in King, with the witch from Romania. The inclination has always been there forever. Now is the time to realize what you are meant to do. Join me."

"I can't." I shook my head. "Mama, I can't."

"Yes. Nell, how long have you been wishing for me? Missing me? Take my hand."

She slid her fingers through mine, and power slammed into me. It wasn't the sweet and compelling link that I felt when I touched Rafe. Instead, it pulsed into me, washing everything in a shade of red. My heart rocked against my ribs, and I wanted nothing but to destroy. Seek, take, destroy. Make it burn, let it all burn ...

I saw the beauty and logic of my mother's plan. The drones were here to make life easier in the short term, and in the long term, they were going to start the revolution. Even now, they were pouring into cities around the world, just waiting for the sign.

And it was all going to burn, and when the world was in ruins, we would be there to take over.

I smiled at my mother, and she gathered me into her arms again.

"Nell."

The bounding around my power dropped away, and I could feel the deep well, just waiting for me to dip in. It made me dizzy. What I could do was limitless. What I would do no longer had any stops.

"Even now, the drones are gathering. They think we're getting ready to go out and save the world. But we're going to have a bon fire instead. The biggest one ever. And you'll be here at my side, Nell. Where you belong."

Nothing existed anymore except the plan. Our goals. The power. It was both the means and the end.

Behind me was a distant echo. I heard my name. It was holding me back from taking the final step. The sound made me pause, calling to a part of me that lay deep within and yet had not yet been buried by the pulsating red haze.

"Nell. Don't do this. This isn't you. You are not that person. You are not your mother."

I faltered. *My mother. Was I my mother? What would I give up to be with her again? What wouldn't I?*

"Nell. Hold onto me. Don't do this. Nell, *I love you.*"

And then there was another energy, a stronger power, and it crashed into the first red power. I cried out as it washed over me, cleaning away the confusion and the beating. It was sweet and loving and I wanted to lie in its embrace forever. This power didn't seek, take and destroy. It loved, and it strengthened, and it made new.

Rafe's hand was on my arm, skin to skin, and his hand was clutching mine, palm to palm. Peace surrounded me, along with an electric blue glow.

"Remember this, Nell. Remember our link. I love you."

I blinked, and the world was crystal clear.

My mother stood a foot away from me. Her face had transformed to a hideous snarl, and her hair was tangled and streaked with gray. Hate filled her eyes.

"*Not mine.*" She raised her hand, and the air stirred. "You made your choice, and you chose poorly, daughter."

She threw back her head and chanted something. The air swirled around us, nearly knocking me from my feet. I grabbed for Rafe, and he held onto me as I hid my face in his shoulder.

But I knew I couldn't let her win, and so even with my eyes screwed tight, I called forth my own wind, a calming force to combat her vortex and asked water to spurt from the ground soaking everything around us. I turned within Rafe's arms, opened my eyes and let loose the torrent of power. Trees toppled, and dirt and debris flew through the air.

My mother screamed, a high-pitched noise that tried to interrupt me. But I only pulled Rafe's hand tighter against mine and closed her mouth.

The two men guarding my mother fought against the on-slaught of wind and trees, heads down and eyes closed. One rushed toward Rafe, but I knocked him away with a glance. He landed on his back with a thud.

"Thanks, baby." Rafe smiled at me.

"Any time."

People poured out of the orchard, some heading toward us, but most trying to get away. There were powers mixed in with those who had none, but I couldn't take the time to sep-arate them now. I sent them sprawling and covered the group with a force that kept them on the ground, paralyzed.

When the noise died and I could only feel my own soft breeze, I lifted my head. The world was wet, with water drip-ping from trees above us. People were crying, but I didn't think anyone was badly injured. I found the man who had been protecting my mother along with the one who had cap-tured Rafe and me. They were pinned to the ground, groan-ing.

But when I looked for my mother, she was gone.

Frantically, I scanned the area. I couldn't find a trace of her power.

"She disappeared." Rafe pulled me to him again and spoke into my ear. "Just vanished while you were wrecking havoc. It's okay. It's over."

I viewed the destroyed camp from over his shoulder. In the shadows, just beyond the edge of the trees, I thought I saw a shadow moving stealthily. It was a man, and he paused as though he felt my eyes on him. When he looked at me, a cold wave of revulsion nearly dragged me under. I caught my breath, but the man vanished before I could say anything.

"Are you all right?" Rafe held me in front of him, studying my face. "What's wrong?"

I clung to him, my lifeline and my link to light.

"Not a thing. Not one thing."

EPILOGUE

WITHIN A FEW MOMENTS, the camp was swarmed with uniformed men. Rafe and I stood to the side. I expected them to detain us for questioning, but for some reason, they didn't seem to even notice us.

I glanced at Rafe and noticed him focusing on the group.

"Nice job, mind bender."

He shrugged. "Well, it's good to know I'm good for something. I'm beginning to feel expendable, hanging around you."

"Never." I stood on my tiptoes and kissed him. "I was close to the edge, Rafe. That was my mother. I mean, you saw her, right? That wasn't just me hallucinating?"

He frowned. "I saw her. But Nell ... I'm not sure. It felt off. I didn't so much see a person as sense a power, something pulling you toward her. It was ... weird. And then she was gone."

"What did she look like to you?" I was shaken, and I needed to know the truth. Had she been here, or had some power used her face, the idea of my mother, to draw me in and tempt me?

"She ... she looked like a witch. I don't mean to say that's what witches look like." He added that last bit hastily, watching my eyes. "Not that you look like that. But her hair was wild and her eyes were ... crazy. For just a minute there, so were yours."

"It would have been so easy." I let myself sink back into that moment. "I was ready to join her. The power was so strong. I wanted it. Every bit of it."

"You didn't though. You resisted." Rafe tightened his arm around me.

I leaned into his chest. "But if it weren't for you, I would have gone with her. She would have sucked me in." I paused, remembering. "Rafe, she said my father lied, set her up. Do you think that's true?"

"I don't know. And maybe that's something you need to ask him."

"Maybe."

We watched the camp come apart as the authorities rounded everyone up, talking to groups and loading others into trucks.

"Did we do it, do you think? By taking down this camp, did we stop this?"

"Well, you definitely slowed them down."

A familiar voice spoke from behind us, and I turned to see Cathryn standing in the mud, looking perfectly groomed in a pink suit and nude pumps, not a hair out of place.

"Boss lady!" Rafe released me and scooped her into a bear hug. She pushed at him half-heartedly, but I thought I saw a gleam of tears in her eyes.

"One time, Rafe. I'll allow that one time. And don't

think that just because you almost got killed and scared us all half out of our minds more than once that I'm going to let you get away with everything."

He grinned at her. "Never."

She shook her head. "Incorrigible, as always. I think you're going to need a nice long session with Zoe when we get back to the Institute."

Cathryn turned to me, and her eyes softened. "Nell, you did it. You have our gratitude and appreciation. Whatever we can do ... whatever you want, it's yours."

"Thank you, Cathryn." I slipped my hand into Rafe's. "A little peace and quiet is all I need right now."

She smiled. "I can understand that. I'm going to need you both to be debriefed as soon as we get you back to Harper Creek, you understand. We've made a major strike here. The men we took are high up in the organization, and they'll be talking to us, I'm sure. But Mallory Jones is still out there. Our work isn't done." She looked at her watch. "I flew up on the Carruthers plane. Can I give you a lift back to Florida?"

Rafe glanced at me, and the side of mouth lifted in the half-smile I loved.

"No, thanks. We've got the Impala here. I think we'll drive home." He pulled me against him so that my back was against his chest. "And Cathryn, don't expect us there right away."

She nodded. "I understand. I'll see you when I see you. Keep in touch, though. We've missed you both." She turned and walked away from us, picking her way through the muck.

I turned in Rafe's arms. "So we've saved the world, for now at least. What's next?"

He wrapped his arms around me and tugged me tighter. "I say, a hotel with a king-sized bed and twenty-four hour room service. How does that sound?"

I threaded my fingers through his hair and pulled his lips down to mine. "I think that sounds heavenly. I say we should stay there for a week."

"Done." He covered his lips with mine, and my body melted, desire rising up to consume us both, the connection between us alive and dancing.

When he came up for breath, Rafe framed my face in his hands. "Did you hear what I said to you, when your mother was trying to pull you in?"

I brushed my fingertips over the sexy scruff on his face. "I did. But don't worry. I won't hold you to it. I know you were trying to save me."

He cocked his head and narrowed his eyes. "I meant it. Every word. You, Nell Massler, are what I want. And I plan on loving you for at least an eternity."

I locked my hands behind his neck and met his dark eyes. "I'm not an easy person, Rafe. I'm demanding, I'm damaged and I carry more baggage than your typical cruise ship."

He grinned. "Do I look worried? And remember, I'm no picnic either. I can match you for damaged baggage. Are you sure you can handle it?"

I pulled his mouth to mine, giving him my answer in the best way I knew. And then I whispered into his ear, the words coming easily for once as I let them flow from my heart.

"You are the first person I've ever desired. You will be the last person I ever desire." I stood back a little, smiling up into his face.

"And remember, I'm one of those annoying people who always gets what she wants."

ACKNOWLEDGMENTS

I have been waiting to write Nell's book for so long that seeing it finished is almost surreal. She was the first character who I knew would have a spin-off book from The King Series, and yet it turned out that Rafe had to come first. Ahem.

As it happens, this neat little two-book set—a duet—is only an introduction to Rafe and Nell's story. There will be more books to come. Be patient.

Shepherding a book from idea to publication is not for the faint of heart. I am fortunate to be surrounded by people much smarter and more talented than myself. Amanda Long and Stacey Blake make it all look and sound better. . .and Stacey makes all my books absolutely beee-yootiful! Her formatting is fabulous.

My promotion helpers, particular Devon Copsey and Melanie Marsh, are awesome. And my PBT/Hayson family, led by Jen Rattie, has been endlessly supportive. All the bloggers who have cheered for these books make me smile. Thank you.

Mandie, thank you for our writing weekend. It was so much fun and relaxing. . .once a quarter, right? Much love to you, always.

Ladies of Romantic Edge Books. . .are we ready to rock?

And of course, oodles of love and thanks to my family, who hasn't seen much of me this year. Thanks for tolerating Mommy's wacky schedule, for stepping up to keep our lives moving and for always being excited with me. I love you to smithereens.

Last but far from least, readers of The King Series who rallied around Rafe (especially Carrie, Molly, Nancy and Carolyn). . .you rock my world. I loved all the notes and emails and messages. I hope you enjoy Nell, too. She could use some friends.

ABOUT THE AUTHOR

Photo: Marilyn Bellinger

Tawdra Thompson Kandle lives in central Florida with her husband, children, cats and dog. She loves homeschooling, cooking, traveling and reading, not necessarily in that order. And yes, she has purple hair.

You can follow Tawdra here…
Facebook:
https://www.facebook.com/AuthorTawdraKandle
Twitter:https://twitter.com/tawdra
Website: tawdrakandle.com

OTHER BOOKS BY THE AUTHOR

The King Series
Fearless
Breathless
Restless
Endless

The Posse

Best Served Cold

Undeniable

ROMANTIC EDGE BOOKS

Meet the authors of Romantic Edge Books: Nine Authors Writing Romance with an Edge

If you have enjoyed UNQUENCHABLE by Tawdra Kandle, here are some other books you may enjoy:

Anthologies
Cupid Painted Blind
Once Upon a Midnight Dreary
Eternal Summer
A Christmas Yet To Come

By Olivia Hardin
Bend-Bite-Shift Trilogy
Witch Way Bends
Bitten Shame
Shifty Business
For Love of Fae Series
Sweet Magic Song
Transcendent
Lynlee Lincoln Series
Trolling for Trouble
Tangled Up In Trouble
Stand Alone Novels
All For Hope

OTHER BOOKS FROM HAYSON PUBLISHING